Dragon Road

GOLDEN MOUNTAIN
CHRONICLES: 1939

Also by
Laurence Yep

Golden Mountain Chronicles

*The extraordinary intergenerational story of the Young family
from Three Willows Village, Kwangtung province,
China, and their lives in the Land of the
Golden Mountain—America.*

The Serpent's Children (1849)
Mountain Light (1855)
Dragon's Gate (1867)
A Newbery Honor Book
The Traitor (1885)
Dragonwings (1903)
A Newbery Honor Book
Dragon Road (1939)
Child of the Owl (1965)
Sea Glass (1970)
Thief of Hearts (1995)

The Dragon's Child
A Story of Angel Island
The Earth Dragon Awakes
The San Francisco Earthquake of 1906
Sweetwater
When the Circus Came to Town

The Dragon Prince
Dream Soul
The Rainbow People
The Imp That Ate My Homework

The Tiger's Apprentice Trilogy
The Tiger's Apprentice
Tiger's Blood
Tiger Magic

Dragon of the Lost Sea Fantasies
Dragon of the Lost Sea
Dragon Steel
Dragon Cauldron
Dragon War

Chinatown Mysteries
The Case of the Goblin Pearls
The Case of the Lion Dance
The Case of the Firecrackers

Edited by Laurence Yep
American Dragons
Twenty-Five Asian American Voices

Awards
Laura Ingalls Wilder Award

LAURENCE YEP

Dragon Road

GOLDEN MOUNTAIN
CHRONICLES: 1939

 HarperCollins*Publishers*

Dragon Road

Copyright © 2008 by Laurence Yep

Library of Congress Cataloging-in-Publication Data

Yep, Laurence, date
    Dragon road / Laurence Yep. — 1st ed.
        p. cm.
    Includes bibliographical references.
    Summary: In 1939, unable to find regular jobs because of the Great Depression,
long-time friends Cal Chin and Barney Young tour the country as members of a
Chinese American basketball team.
    ISBN 978-0-06-027520-4 (trade bdg.) — ISBN 978-0-06-027521-1 (lib. bdg.)
    1. Chinese Americans—Fiction. [1. Chinese Americans—Fiction. 2. Basketball—
Fiction. 3. Depressions—1939—Fiction. 4. United States—History—20th cen-
tury—Fiction.] I. Title.
    PZ7.Y44Dqk 2008   2008000784
    [Fic]—dc22   CIP
                                                                                AC

Typography by Andrea Vandergrift
1 2 3 4 5 6 7 8 9 10

First Edition

To Wong Buck Hong, George Lee,
Sonny Lee, Chauncey Yip, Fred Gok,
and Hing Tai Sun of the Hong Wah Kues,
and to Franche Yep of the Mei Wahs,
and, of course, to Thomas Yep

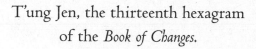

T'ung Jen, the thirteenth hexagram
of the *Book of Changes*.

"Brotherhood opens new worlds."

PREFACE

In 1939 and 1940, a professional Chinese American basketball team, the Hong Wah Kues, barnstormed across America and Canada, taking on all comers. Chinatowners from that time still speak about them with pride.

While this novel is based on that pioneering team, I want to stress that it is fiction and all the characters are my own creation.

Readers will probably also need some notes on basketball as it was played in 1939. There was a jump ball at center court after every basket, and though colleges had decided to do away with it, this had yet to be adopted by many professional teams. When everyone did, the effect was to speed up games and increase the scores.

Another rule change required teams to bring the ball

across a line in the middle of the court in ten seconds or turn the ball over. However, after crossing the line, there was no twenty-four-second clock that required a shot at the basket, so the possessing team could stall as long as they liked. At the time, it was also legal to knock away a shot as it came down toward the basket, though since then this has become illegal goaltending.

The local sports hero Hank Luisetti is famous for having introduced the running one-handed shot, which let him shoot over taller opponents, so that he broke the national scoring record. Up until then, players used a slower, more deliberate two-handed set shot.

PART ONE

Chinatown

CHAPTER | I

Autumn, 1939

W hen I left Chinatown that morning, I never expected to be running for my life. I'd like to blame the trouble on my pal Barney Young, but the con had been my idea in the first place.

When I was a kid, I'd listened to Grandpa Joe, Barney's grandfather. He said study hard and I'd get ahead. So I got straight As.

My good-for-nothing dad said I was a chump for doing that. But I told him to take a hike. Who listens to a rummy anyway?

It turned out, though, that he was right. The whole world had been deep in the Depression for years—I don't mean the emotional kind. There were no jobs, no money, and stores and factories had closed everywhere. When I graduated from high school in '38, the newspapers were all bragging America was coming out of it, but you could have fooled me. In Chinatown there were fifty guys lined up for any one job.

About the only other thing that Barney and I were good at was basketball, and our teams had torn up the Chinatown tournaments. However, no one knew us outside of Chinatown. Barney's grades had been lousy in Galileo High School, and I'd been kicked off the basketball team in high school after the "incident"—which was fine by me. Who needed some coach telling me how to play basketball? Basketball just is. It's in your guts, not your head.

I figured we could go to playgrounds outside of Chinatown and con some guys into playing for money.

Barney thought it was pretty harebrained—and a little scary too because when Chinese left Chinatown, they never knew what might happen.

So Barney wasn't too crazy about leaving Chinatown, but he was just as desperate as me. We gathered up all the medals and trophies from the Chinatown tournaments and pawned them. Three shelf-loads of honors only got us two bucks, but that was all we needed. Barney cut up some newspaper, and we slapped a dollar on the top and the bottom. That gave us a money roll to tempt the marks into a game.

Then we scooted up to the Italian area above Chinatown called North Beach. Chinese could expect a fight there about 50 percent of the time. But we set up in a school playground anyway. We missed baskets. We lost dribbles.

When these Italian guys came in, they tried to drive us off the court. But we challenged them to a game. On an inspiration, I began to talk in broken English, and Barney picked up his cue and fractured his English too. And we hammed it up like the way Americans thought Chinese acted.

Oh, and that was the beauty of the scam. We couldn't have fooled them if they hadn't already fooled themselves about Chinese in general.

They figured they'd teach us a lesson, so we started to play. We pretended to be awful, so when the money roll "accidentally" fell out of my pocket, the chumps licked their chops and suggested we play for cash.

We took them for five bucks, and once the bet was down, they licked their chops like the cat that ate the canary. One of the jokers even began to hum "China Boy," which had been a popular tune a few years before.

So it was a real pleasure to turn the tables on them. They stuck their arms up high but didn't move them around—which was their idea of defense. Up until that moment, we'd been shooting just like them and like most everyone who played basketball. To do a standard shot, shooters came to a stop, set up, and took their sweet time throwing the ball at the basket. It was a slow, methodical—and boring—process.

"Now?" Barney asked me with a wink.

"Now," I agreed. There was this Italian kid Hank Luisetti, also from North Beach, who had invented a running one-handed shot. His Stanford team had stormed through the big college tournament back east, the Basketball Writers Association Tournament. I'd snuck into a game down on the Farm, as the Stanford campus was called, and fallen in love with that shot at first sight. I'd never seen anyone shoot so fast. It caught most everyone by surprise.

I started to dribble on the run around the boneheads. That sent them scooting backward to take new positions. Then I gave a little jump into the air and whipped the ball up by my right ear, thrusting the ball with my right hand upward and outward. As I rose almost to their height, I could see the ball arcing smoothly toward the basket.

As the ball swished through the net, their jaws dropped open. I guess they never expected me to know or use Hank's shot.

It was a sweet moment when they got this funny look in their eyes and realized they'd been wrong about us. But that only made them madder, because they figured they were taller and could still take us. Height, though, is a disadvantage when you're just plain clumsy, so it was easy to snatch the ball from them.

Barney and I scooted in and out and all around them, like they were mannequins, while we hit basket after basket. Barney could hit Hank's shot too, but he was more accurate with the traditional shooting methods; and that was fine because he could always get into the clear to take his time.

So they starting calling us sly slit-eyes and other rotten names, so I guess we'd moved from one stereotype to another: from bumbling immigrants to cunning Fu Man Chus.

Barney looked worried and whispered to me not to blow my top. When we were little kids, it had been stiffs just like them who had made fun of us in school—pulling up the corners of their eyes so they slanted and making funny singsong noises and then saying rotten things.

I'd always gotten mad, not so much at the words, but because they thought of me as some sort of cartoon and not a person. Of course, they only baited me when there was a pack of them, but I'd take a swing anyway, and poor Barney would wind up at my side because that was the sort of guy he was. We'd be standing back to back, fighting for our lives—and getting beaten up too.

My anger had gotten me kicked off the high school team. When I'd shown up, the first string guard started saying things not only about me but also about Chinatown and all Chinese just for good measure. I'd decked him. Okay, so I deserved some sort of punishment but so did he for saying those things. But the point guard had been the nephew of a teacher, and they'd gone straight to the principal, so I'd wound up being banned from all sports.

I just grinned at Barney, though. "Don't worry," I winked. "I got my temper under control."

Now, we were getting even by cheating them, so I let their insults just roll off my back.

The losers were still cursing as Barney and I left them and swaggered back to Chinatown. The money had made us flush. You could get a whole steamed chicken for ten cents at the Celestial Forest and all the tea you could drink and all the rice you could eat as well, so our winnings could have filled our bellies for a long time. But we blew it on a ten-course banquet for us and our girls, both of whom were named Jean. It could have been confusing, but Barney's girlfriend, for whom he was head over heels, was nicknamed Tiger. When we were small, Barney had been teasing her in the school yard and she'd bitten him. It had taken the teacher to pry her jaws loose. Barney was real sweet on Tiger, but I was really just pals with Jean.

After that, Barney and I pulled the scam real regular. It didn't bother my conscience in the least, because we couldn't have cheated them if they hadn't wanted to cheat us in the first place.

We always blew what we won, but we didn't worry. The city was full of pushovers. We usually spent it on our girls, but sometimes Barney, whose conscience would bother him every now and then, would give some to his grandfather, Grandpa Joe, who didn't earn much as the secretary at the Chinatown YMCA. Sometimes my old man swiped my dough from me to buy more booze.

I could never do things by halves, so I studied the real Chinese immigrants to pull off the hoax better: I straightened up my posture, cut down on my gestures, listened to how they mangled English words and sentences until I could have passed for someone who was fresh off the boat.

We'd pulled the con so often in North Beach and the Western Addition and the Mission that we'd had to strike out for greener pastures, like Butchertown in the southeast part of San Francisco. There the wind blew from the stockyard, so the air stunk of cattle and blood.

We tried not to choke on the stench as we began to throw the ball around in the school yard—and dropping it more times than we caught it. You know, pretending to be overconfident and not aware of how goofy we looked. Finally, a couple of Butcher boys came into the yard; they'd figured to take us for a few bucks.

But keeping up the scam was real hard because they were so lousy. They handled the basketball like it was a melon; and when one of them tried to drive me, the basketball just seemed to float in the air and whisper to me, "Don't let this fathead manhandle me, Flash. Save me."

So I swiped it.

When the big lummox went down, I started to grin, but Barney slashed a finger across his throat to can it. So

I put on my serious, schoolboy face again and kept right on dribbling the basketball. Behind me I heard the sap hollering, "Foul. That was a foul. You tripped me!"

The goon was so clumsy he'd stumbled over his own two feet, so I was going to argue but Barney muttered, "Ix-nay, Cal. Ix-nay. We're still setting them up, and if we handle these two right, we can get the ante up to a saw-buck." (We only had two bucks to our name—but no matter. We'd win.) Ten bucks would let us treat our girls to a show and dinner.

So I stopped and waited for the mauler to get to his feet, and then I threw him the ball, looking awkward on purpose. It was hard not to grin when the lunkhead missed the free throw.

The lunkhead's partner charged past Barney, plodding on his feet like an ox. He palmed the rebound easily in one meat hook of a hand. He was a big guy in a shirt still stained with cattle blood, and his hands were so big I bet he didn't even need a sledgehammer to do in a cow. He could just clobber it with one of his fists.

"Foul," I said, making it sound more like "Four."

He sneered as I moved over to guard him. "I don't see any blood."

Barney spread his hands. "Him, me, no want trouble." Barney always played the Goody Two-shoes while I played the hothead.

Hammer Hand dribbled toward the basket, moving

so slow I could have snatched the ball away a couple of times, but we let them have an easy shot. When he missed, though, I groaned inside. It was going to take work to let these clowns think they were winning.

As the fathead cut in for the rebound, he tried to hip me. But he telegraphed it so much that it was easy to sidestep. The real hard part was to make it look unintentional.

Barney hopped around, swinging his arms but not in any way that could block a shot, and the chump made it.

We let the Butchers get up by eight baskets—though it wasn't easy. All the time I kept on protesting and whining while I pretended to be clumsy. It worked so well that the Butchers proposed a bet of twenty bucks. "I know you got the scratch."

I pretended not to know what he meant. "What this 'scratch'?"

He held up one paw, palm upward, and pretended it had an itch. "You know. The stuff that cures the itch. Denaro. Shekels. Moola. Filthy lucre."

His partner elbowed him. "He don't know what you're talking about, dopey." He faced me. "You know, mo-ney?" He exaggerated the last two syllables for my benefit. "Sabe me?"

"I sabe," I said, and pointed at him. "You, scratch, too?"

It was the day after payday, so Big Hand still had a wad of his own. (We'd deliberately picked this time of the week to go hunting—right when the bushes were ripe with moneyberries.) But we'd never played for such high stakes before.

Maybe I reached for it a little too eagerly because the pigeon suddenly got suspicious. "I want to check your money again."

I thought the jig was up because all they'd see was a wad of cut-up newspaper with a dollar wrapped on each side. So I started searching for the gate out of the school yard. Unfortunately, we'd let the goons get between it and us. We were going to get pounded.

"Let me hold the stakes," a voice said.

A man in his twenties stood there in a real spiffy suit—made by a tailor and not off the Emporium rack. He was tall for a Chinese, but the redheaded American who was with him was even taller. He was an old geezer— already in his late thirties—and had a slight limp.

"Why should we trust you?" the sap demanded.

Mr. Spiffy reached a hand up to the Redhead's shoulder. "Because I'll put my friend up as collateral."

Hammer Hand squinted at the Redhead. "You look familiar."

"Could be," the Redhead said. "I used to play for the Celtics." He talked fast like he wanted to make sure he got out everything he had to say before anyone could cut him off. The New York Celtics were a professional team that beat everyone in sight. I have no ear for accents, but he sure sounded like he came from New York.

He had the height for playing basketball, and he was dressed in a suit just as nifty as Mr. Spiffy's.

"No kidding," the jerk said, impressed. "What's your monicker?"

"Jack," the Redhead said. One corner of his mouth twisted up in a smirk—like he knew a secret joke that no one else knew. "Jack Coughlan."

"I follow what's been happening in New York," Hammer Hand squinted suspiciously. "And I ain't never heard that name."

"I got injured about twelve years ago," Coughlan said.

He seemed annoyed that none of us recognized his name. And the rubes were reluctant to hand over the money to two strangers. Suddenly the chump let out a whistle. "Hey, Nuncio. Over here. You got to hold some stakes for us."

I turned to see four even beefier guys head inside the yard. This was changing the odds against us.

"We not trust friends," I said. "Bet off."

"When you're down two baskets from winning, kid?" Hammer Hand glared. "You know what we do to welchers?"

Probably what they did to cows in the slaughterhouse. I gulped.

"We're neutral because we don't know any of you," Mr.

Spiffy said, holding out his hand. "Let us hold it. And your friends can make sure we don't run off with it."

Hammer Hand scratched his head with one of his big paws, but he handed the money over. "Play you next after we teach these twerps a lesson."

"They could use it," Coughlan said, and glanced at his friend. "This is a waste."

"We'll see," Mr. Spiffy said.

"We don't have the time," Coughlan complained.

"You said you'd let me manage this part," Mr. Spiffy said. He flipped through the chumps' money. "It's all here." Then he snapped the fingers of his free hand at Barney. "Let's go, kid. Unless you're waiting for your dough to have babies."

With no choice, Barney handed over his roll. I tensed my legs, getting ready to make a break for it. But Mr. Spiffy thumbed through Barney's fake roll. "It's okay."

I stared at him, but Mr. Spiffy just jerked his head at me. "Better get back on the court, kid, unless you expect your partner to win by himself."

As I trotted toward the others I tried to figure out what their angle was. First of all, what were two well-dressed gents doing in a Butchertown school yard? And why were they saving our bacon?

When I joined Barney at half-court, he glanced at the friends nervously. "What do we do?"

"Win and then scoot," I said. "Don't even try to get back your stake."

"But those two bucks is all we got," Barney complained.

"A cracked skull will cost you more," I said.

I figured it was smarter to get this over as quick as possible. I took the inbounds pass from Barney, dribbled through the two pigeons like they were trees, and made an easy little bank shot.

When we made the next two baskets just as fast, I heard muttering from off court. The pushovers' friends were glowering, already suspecting a trick. Mr. Spiffy was still there, just smiling, but Coughlan was gone.

And then I forgot about them, or our worries, and I just turned it loose. It was like the old days when I was playing at Gal. Some games I'd felt like a shark slicing through the ocean. And there'd even been a few games when playing basketball was the closest thing to flying. With nothing to win, I could give up playing the fake game and play my own now.

It was the kind of basketball I loved. Two more baskets and the boneheads gave up trying to play the game. They tried to punch, kick, and trip us, but it didn't matter. They were just nuisances on our way to the hoop. And when Barney made the winning basket, not only the idiots but also their friends headed right for us.

One of the friends glared at me. "Now I remember. You're Flash Chin. I played against you a long time ago in junior high." He shouted to the others. "Hey, guys, he's a ringer. That's Flash Chin."

"Go," I said, but Barney was already hightailing it for the school gates. My legs were not only great for jumping but also for running—especially from a mob of angry marks. For a moment, we were dodging fists and feet. It was like trying to walk through Union Square when all the pigeons fly up at once all around you. Then we were out on the street.

"Which way?" Barney asked.

"I don't remember," I panted in a panic.

By now we knew escape routes all over San Francisco, but we hadn't had a chance to learn Butchertown's lay-out yet and our pursuers did.

Suddenly a Studebaker roared up and Coughlan shouted through the open window. "Hop in, boys."

Even so, we hesitated. What was his game?

"Follow me, boys," Mr. Spiffy said as he darted past. "They're right on my heels."

If the chuckleheads could run as fast as they cursed, they would have caught us by now. Even so, they'd reached the gates.

"Let's go," I said, jerking Barney's arm. Mr. Spiffy had pulled the rear door open, and Barney plunged right through it and I went after him. Mr. Spiffy shoved in after us, and Coughlan took off even before the door was shut.

The other idiots just stood and swore and waved their fists, but Hammer Hand actually tried to chase us, coughing in the exhaust as he tried to swear.

Mr. Spiffy leaned forward. "Don't tease him. You're the one who said we didn't have time to waste."

"I just thought he needed the exercise," Coughlan said, but he picked up speed, leaving Hammer Hand far behind.

"Your winnings," Mr. Spiffy tossed the chumps' stake into my lap. "And your trash." He dumped Barney's fake wad after it.

After Barney and I rearranged ourselves against the upholstered seat, we divvied up the money. As I stowed my share away, I asked, "Who are you?"

"Two gentlemen with a proposition," Coughlan said.

I figured they had an angle. Everyone does. I guess people were like that before the Depression. But now with so many people without jobs, it brought the larceny out in most people—except for Grandpa Joe. "We're not interested. We're doing just great."

"Yeah," Barney chimed in. "We just had our biggest pay-off, so you can drop us off at the nearest trolley stop."

Coughlan glanced over his shoulder. "You call that a payoff? You should have taken them for everything they were worth. Always go for the throat before they can."

I thought I was tough, but maybe Coughlan was pit-bull vicious, so I didn't want to have anything to do with him. "Thanks, I'll put your pearls of wisdom in the next fortune cookie."

Coughlan steered around a double-parked car, an old flivver. "Do you want to spend all your life wasting your talents, cheating working stiffs out of nickels and dimes?"

There was a button on the upholstery that was digging into my back and I wriggled my shoulders, trying to find a more comfortable position. "It's none of your business."

"We just saved your skin," Coughlan said.

"Who asked you to?" I said.

"Let's hear them out," Barney said, stashing away the money carefully out of Mr. Spiffy's reach. I doubted, though, that they were going to roll us for twenty-two bucks.

"I'm organizing a basketball team," Coughlan said.

"*We're* organizing," Mr. Spiffy corrected him, and then said to us. "All Chinese Americans, and we'll barnstorm across the country."

"Barnstorming?" Barney asked.

"It's what they call those traveling aviators who put on shows around the country," Coughlan explained. "After World War One, some of those fliers couldn't give up the sky. They got some surplus airplanes and began to go around doing tricks and selling rides to the rubes. I hear one of those tricks was to fly through a barn, so they got the nickname barnstormers."

They weren't con men. They were crazy . . . and Barney told them so before I could.

"You want to play for small change all your life, stay here," Coughlan laughed. "But if you want to make real money, come with us."

I thought about the reaction of all the mugs we'd scammed. "What makes you think people will pay to see Chinese?"

"They pay to see Negroes," Coughlan said. "You ever hear of the Rens?"

"Yeah, I heard of the Renaissance," I said. They were an all-Negro team from New York and the best in the whole country, from what the sports writers said.

"And then there's the Harlem Globetrotters"— Coughlan grinned—"who are actually from the play-grounds of Chicago."

"Then why do they say they're from Harlem?" I asked.

"Because the owner's this slick guy name of Saperstein," Coughlan said. "He figured that folks'd pay better if they thought his team came from New York too. I'll leave the playing to you. You leave the thinking to me."

Mr. Spiffy frowned. "But we're going to give the crowd the real deal: Chinese from San Francisco."

Barney leaned over me to stare at him. "You look familiar."

"My Chinatown team almost won the city champion-ship," Mr. Spiffy said expectantly.

Barney snapped his fingers. "Topper Tom."

Topper pretended to set a top hat on his head. "That's me."

I thought Mr. Spiffy had looked familiar, but I'd

only seen him in a basketball uniform before this. Topper Tom had captained basketball teams that scorched the tournaments. They'd called themselves the Chinese All Stars.

"I'm Barney Young." Barney jerked a thumb at me. "And this is Calvin Chin."

"I know. I saw some of your games in the Chinatown tournaments," Topper said to Barney and then nodded at me. "That's why we've been searching for you. But you're both hard to find."

I eyed his fancy duds. "Maybe you spent too much time in a tailor shop."

"You got some potential, kid," Coughlan said. "You're fast. Is that how you got your nickname? Like Flash Gordon? Like that comic strip."

Topper knew the Chinatown gossip though. "No, it's for his temper." He made a fist and then spread his fingers wide, pantomiming an explosion. "He flashes like dynamite."

Grandpa Joe, who'd worked in a coal mine in Wyoming when he was a kid, had said I'd reminded him of a powder keg.

"You didn't come slumming to get our autographs," I said.

"No, like I said, we've got a team that's going to play games across the country," Topper said. "You guys could be on it."

I gave Topper another look over. He looked trim, and judging by his sprint to the car, I knew he was fit.

"If you got your team, what do you need us for?" I asked.

"One of our guys went back to China to fight the Japanese," Topper explained. The Japanese had invaded China two years ago. "And the other bum got married and his wife won't let him go on the road."

"You make it sound like a crime to get hitched," I said.

"He let down the team," Topper said with a shake of his head. "That is a crime."

Barney, though, had only one thing on his mind. "We'd get to travel all over the country?" he asked eagerly.

"After eighty games, you'll see more of every state and every territory than you'll want to," Coughlan laughed.

"But you'll see it from the bench," I told Barney indignantly. "You were a starter."

"In Chinatown tournaments," Topper said, "but those were just sideshows. With us, you'd be in the Big Tent."

"Forget it," I said. "I don't like splinters in my behind."

Barney elbowed me. "But we could get out of Chinatown."

That was tempting. I'd never been farther south than Concepcion and never farther north than a hike in Mill

23

Valley. But I had my pride. Nowadays that was all I had. "We're not tourists."

"No," Topper snapped, "you're two twerps stuck in Chinatown all your lives." That hit home a little more than I liked.

Barney didn't want to give up on the idea. "We'd get three squares a day?"

"And a salary." Topper nodded. "There's an accountant who wants to become the Sports Czar of the Pacific. He'll front the money."

Coughlan chimed in, "I'm . . . we are offering a hundred dollars a month while we're on tour."

"But," Topper warned and ticked off the items, "you'll have to pay for your own shoes, meals, and rooms."

The average Joe would have been happy to make a buck a day, so that gave me pause, but it could've been a penny a day for all Barney cared. His eyes got as big as saucers. "Wow, I've never been out of the city limits."

As much as I wanted to believe it, the deal sounded just too good to be true. "We're better off staying here," I said to Barney.

"Doing what?" Topper asked bluntly. "Cheating blockheads on the playground?"

That stung my pride. I was no loafer. "It's not like we haven't looked. But there's ten guys fighting for just the chance to wash dishes."

Barney nudged me excitedly. When he sank his

teeth into something, he couldn't let go. "We'd get to see America, Cal."

My old man blew out enough hot air for me to recognize a pipe dream when I heard one. "It won't work," I said, shaking my head. "You'll wind up broke in the middle of some desert town."

"Broke is broke," Barney argued, "whether it's in Chinatown or somewhere else."

"I'm not interested," I said flatly.

"I'll talk to Cal," Barney promised. I knew he wouldn't go without me, his partner.

"We're holding practice at the Japantown Y gym tomorrow at seven o'clock," Topper said. "You can try out then."

"You want us just to try out for the bench?" I asked angrily.

"It's the Big Tent," Topper reminded me. "Look, kid. You going to hide in Chinatown all your life? Is the biggest adventure in your life going to be taking a trolley to Butchertown? There's more to the world than Chinatown and San Francisco."

Barney chewed on the idea like a dog on a bone and added, "And get paid for it."

Part of me wanted to wipe that superior smile off Topper's face. I was tempted to win the tryouts and then tell him what he could do with his offer, but that would be playing his game. And I always played my own. "Don't hold your breath," I muttered.

CHAPTER | II

Coughlan cruised up Third Street to Market. There were panhandlers everywhere as well as apple sellers—out-of-work stiffs, too proud to beg, who sold apples on the sidewalk. The most enterprising had rolled up a sheet of paper into a megaphone and was crooning "Brother, Can You Spare a Dime" like Rudy Vallee as he tried to peddle his fruit. Even he didn't have any takers.

Coughlan pulled into the curb. "Look at the poor saps, boys. They'd kill for a job cleaning out toilets, and we're offering you the world on a silver platter."

As we got out, Barney nudged me. "You're just too suspicious, Cal."

"And there was never a rainbow you didn't chase," I griped, watching them drive away.

"Boy, someone got out on the wrong side of bed this morning," Barney said. We headed over to a cigarette stand and broke the twenty.

The panhandlers and apple sellers converged on us like flies to honey. I shook my head like I didn't understand English. Barney spoke Chinese back to them until, one by one, they gave up in disgust.

As we turned up Grant Avenue, Barney said, "We almost got our heads handed back to us today. Maybe it's time to put the con to rest."

"That's easy for you to say," I said. "You can always go to Grandpa Joe when you're broke. Don't you get tired of sponging off him?"

"You're just jealous," Barney shrugged.

Maybe I was, but I wouldn't admit it to him. Instead, I kept my trap shut and stared ahead.

Barney never could hold a grudge for long. "You know he'd help you out more too, if you just asked. You're a child of a classmate."

That's what our grandfathers had called one another after they had built the railroad. They'd constructed bridges across canyons and dug holes straight through mountains with nothing much more than chisels and hammers and shovels. A lot of their friends had lost their lives, so the survivors called themselves schoolmates because in the old days in China, the men who passed the grueling government exams called one another classmates.

"I've already taken too much." I jammed my hands into my pants. The eleven bucks was burning a hole in my pocket. Maybe I'd go see Jean. Jean was always telling me to save it and make it last. She had a great head for business and numbers and had aced all the commercial classes at Galileo. She would have turned ten dollars into fifty if she had it, but she always gave her money to her big family.

If I could keep my old man from stealing my dough, I could eat for a month, but I never felt so good as when I made Jean smile. She was smart enough to be a doctor or a teacher or run a corporation, but her family could barely manage to feed themselves, let alone pay the tuition for college. She was in the same boat as me: Her grades hadn't gotten her any jobs either.

Still, she was an athlete as well as a bookworm. I'd met her back in junior high. She and some of her gal pals had been playing on the basketball court, so Barney, me, and some of the guys challenged them. The winner would get the court. We had to play by girls' rules—with the court divided into three areas, and teams of six players with two in each section. You couldn't leave your part of the court, and you were only allowed one dribble too.

It took a while to get used to girls' rules, but we were starting to win. "Think you're hot stuff, don't you?" Jean asked me. She was tall for a girl and, as I found out, as tricky as me.

"I know it," I said. I started to reach up for the pass and the next thing I knew I was flat on my back staring up at the sky. And she was throwing the ball down the court.

"You asked for it," I warned her.

She just winked.

The next time we went for a layup. I was going to hip her out of the way, but she just twisted to the side so I missed. Her hands grabbed the ball and as we were coming down her foot just "happened" to knock mine from underneath me, and I landed on the asphalt again. "Somebody must have put on his clumsy shoes this morning." She grinned and passed the ball to a waiting teammate.

I swore that, girl or not, I was going to get even, but I never managed to lay a hand, hip, or foot on her. On the other hand, she flattened me three more times.

With Jean outplaying me, the girls wound up winning, and all the guys looked as bruised and scraped as I did. We limped and crawled over to the bench while the girls began to play a second game.

"Here," she said and tossed me a jar of lion salve, which all of Chinatown swore cured everything from chest colds and rashes to sprained ankles and rheumatism. "This'll ease the ache."

I found myself laughing. "Not to my pride. My name's Flash Chin."

"Jean," she said.

Outside the fence, we were being watched by a bunch of old-timers. They had been born in China and the Americans wouldn't allow them to bring their families here, so they had worked alone in the Land of the Golden Mountain—as they had dubbed America—and sent their money back to their kin in China. Though they probably spent most of their lives here, they still thought of their stay as only temporary, calling themselves "Guests" of the Golden Mountain.

The Guests shook their heads and talked loudly in Chinese about the decline of morals of the young. In their day, boys and girls would never have played a game like that together. But I didn't care. It was 1933 now, so it was up to them to catch up with the times.

But now when Barney and I reached the southern edge of Chinatown, I heard the roar of the crowd and the sound of a trumpet blaring out marching music. Big drums, the kind used for lion dances, were thudding to the same beat.

It wasn't New Year's or any other holiday, so we figured it had to be another War Parade. Last year Japan had invaded China and was still grabbing big chunks of territory. Some kids who'd graduated with me from Gal had even gone back to China to fight the invaders. And Chinatown raised money every chance it got for the cause. Lately the Chinatown newspapers were full of headlines about the new offensive that the Chinese had begun against the Japanese. According to the local rags, China was going to drive the Japanese army into the sea any day now.

Cars were backing up on the side streets trying to get into Grant Avenue, which the cops had shut off. I heard drummers and buglers playing war songs, and I saw the gigantic Chinese flag a few blocks away coming toward us. It was stretched across and parallel to the entire street like a red, white, and blue blanket, held aloft on the edges by marching patriots, some of them in Chinese robes. The sun, shining through the material, turned the street underneath red, white, and blue and colored the marchers.

People on the street dug into their pockets to toss in whatever change they had, and from the windows of the apartments on either side came a rain of more coins. Some donors had more generosity than aim, so it was good to duck into a doorway if you could. Any stray money usually got picked up and tossed into the flag. Its middle was sagging under the weight of all the money contributions.

The spectators were going crazy too, cheering themselves hoarse, but all I was feeling was hungry. The smell of fresh bread was heavy in the air. Johnny Kan must have baked some of his five-cent loaves at Fong and Fong's. The delicious scent mixed with the aroma of the fresh coffee roasting down at the Hills Brothers' factory on the Embarcadero. Before we'd started pulling the con, I'd tried to fool my empty belly by sniffing the smells from the two places. Now, I could buy some with the money we had in our pockets.

Barney's stomach was growling and he rubbed it. "I'm getting some bread and coffee and maybe find some peace and quiet where I can enjoy them."

"Where's your patriotism?" I teased.

Barney turned east. "I can sing 'The Star Spangled Banner' with the best of them. Old Glory's my flag, not that one. I'm an American."

All our lives the Guests had been trying to pound into our heads that we were Chinese, but as far as we were concerned China was just another foreign country that we'd never see, nothing but a question on a geography test.

"I'm going to enjoy the free show," I said, so we split up there with him walking farther into Chinatown and me staying on the edge of Chinatown where Japanese Americans had opened up souvenir shops. I doubted if the tourists could tell the difference between Japanese and Chinese stuff, and I couldn't blame the owners who were just trying to make a buck.

As the flag passed, a breeze lifted a loose dollar bill and sent it floating toward me. I snatched it, aware of the oncoming crowd watching me. So I made a big show of balling it up in my fingers and tossing it back into the flag. Everyone cheered, and I just grinned.

However, a few of the patriots were feeling their oats that day. Some of the crowd paused by a Japanese-owned store and began to shout insults inside. Then I saw an old-timer step in front of the doorway to block them. "Leave them alone. They haven't done anything to you," he scolded.

It was Grandpa Joe, up to his old habits. Some people called him the Conscience of Chinatown; other people just called him the pest. There was never a lost cause that he didn't get sucked into.

He was tricked out in a blue three-piece suit with a gray hat perched on his head. He was only of medium height, but there wasn't a heart bigger in Chinatown. He was involved in almost every cause and charity, and anyone down on their luck could hit him up for fifty cents. Despite my words to Barney, I hit him up myself every now and then.

Except, at the moment, the crowd was too caught up with patriotic fervor to remember all his good deeds.

"Yeah?" a young buck named Zack Jeh threw back. "Well, I hear the Japanese government pays their rent and everything so they can drive the Chinese shops out of business."

Zack was dressed like Joe College in a sporty zippered wool sweater, pants with twenty-two-inch cuffs, and brown oxfords. As I sized up his round face and soft hands, I figured he'd never done a lick of work in his life.

I bet his mama even combed his hair for him every day before she let him leave the house.

"That's just a crazy rumor," Grandpa Joe said. "The Imperial Japanese government has more important things on their minds than ruining some Chinatown shops."

From inside, the storekeeper put on a record of "Chinatown, My Chinatown" and began to play it loud—maybe in the forlorn hope that he could prove he was one of us.

"Why are you sticking up for the enemy?" another of the patriots demanded. The crowd was quickly turning into an angry mob, but that didn't stop Grandpa Joe. When he saw something that wasn't right, he just had to step in. He was either the bravest man I'd ever met or the dumbest. Maybe it was a little of both.

Lately, the newspapers had been full of the atrocities the Japanese were committing in China, so feeling was running higher than ever in Chinatown; I didn't like the looks on the mob's faces.

So against my better judgment, I sidled in next to Zack, who liked to think he was the leader of the outfit. "Cheese it, the cops," I hissed. "I saw them around the corner. There were bunches of Black Marias, too, to haul off plenty of folks."

"So what? We're just speaking our minds," Zack said.

It didn't seem the time to tell him that it shouldn't take long because their brains were probably the size of peanuts. "It's no skin off my nose if you get arrested," I shrugged. "But I hear the jail's got some empty cells, and that always makes the cops look bad because maybe the politicians think they're not doing their jobs. So wouldn't the cops like to fill the clink with Chinese. But me, I'm getting far from here."

It made Zack hesitate because Mama wouldn't have liked to find her baby boy in the hoosegow. All he needed was a distraction. "Up the Chinese," I shouted in Chinese and, taking ten dollars out of my pocket and holding it up so everyone could see, I wadded it up and threw it toward the flag. That was hard to do because that was a hundred dinners at the Celestial Forest, but the sacrifice was for Grandpa Joe.

"Up the Chinese," Zack agreed and punched a fist into the air. And he started after the flag, taking the rest of his nitwits with him.

Out of the corner of my eye, I saw the Japanese storekeeper in the doorway. Now that the crowd had passed, he'd come out from behind his counter. I thought about hitting him up for something, but before I could, he slammed his door shut and flipped the sign so it said CLOSED.

"Not even a thank-you," I grunted.

"Is that why you did it?" Grandpa Joe asked.

"It's certainly not why you did it." I sighed.

He put his hand on my arm. "How have you been?"

"Okay," I said.

He stared down the street after the flag. "Sometimes people can do such wrong things for the right reasons." Even though the mob had been one step away from beating him to a pulp, he seemed to feel sorry for them.

I tried to explain how the world really worked. "Sure, but people don't appreciate being told that." I tapped my head. "You got to use this."

"But you have to listen to this"—Grandpa Joe patted his heart—"when it tells you something is right to do. We're all connected. Chinese say a man and a woman, who are destined to marry, are connected by an invisible string. But it's the same for everybody. Them, us, and him." He waved a hand back at the storekeeper peering at us suspiciously from behind his door. "I just have to remind them."

If anyone else had said that, I would have said they were full of baloney, but I loved Grandpa Joe. Still I had my limits. That's why, even if Grandpa Joe had room for me, I couldn't stay with him. We would have wound up arguing about stuff.

So I changed the subject to something safer. "Barney and me just got the craziest job offer," I laughed. "We can turn pro and play basketball."

It was the wrong thing to say, though, because Grandpa Joe looked worried. "That's crazy. How can grown men make money playing a children's game? But it's just the kind of wild scheme my grandson would believe. Who told you this anyway?"

"One of them was Topper Tom," I said.

"Oh, Topper," Grandpa said with a slow nod. "I remember when the Y introduced the game in Chinatown. Even though he was small, he was so much better than the big boys. He's pretty practical, so maybe there's some truth to it." He lowered his head and studied me from underneath his eyebrows. "But don't do this for the money."

I knew that was Grandpa Joe's personal philosophy. He had the smarts to make a fortune in business, but he was satisfied with his little salary while he scribbled away at night.

"You need dough if you want to eat," I said.

He fixed me with a stare that used to make me squirm when I was small—even now I had to fight down that urge. "You do this for yourself," he said. "You do this because it's what you do well." Suddenly he started to cough. He'd gotten that rattle from the Wyoming coal mine where he had worked as a kid.

"You okay?" I slapped him on the back. "Well, I'm not chasing some pie in the sky. Who'd keep your head from getting broke?"

He nodded silently. He wasn't like the Guests because he'd been born here. He took out a handkerchief and used that instead of spitting on the sidewalk as a Guest would have done.

"I got tape to keep my noggin together," he joked, but then he surprised me. "Still, it might be good if you got out of Chinatown. I'll ask around, and if this is a real opportunity, I think you should take it."

I looked at him in surprise and then shook my head. "The only time I left San Francisco was when you sent me down to Uncle Quail in Concepcion."

He waved an arm. "It's in your blood to travel. The stick-in-the-muds stayed home in China. But your family came all the way across the ocean to the Land of the Golden Mountain. And when they didn't find wealth, they kept going because they were looking for that gold mountain."

"And got shot or lynched. I paid attention to your stories," I said. "You trying to get rid of me?"

"Not after all the work I put in taking care of you," he said, pausing as he read my mind. His kindly eyes regarded me. "I'll keep an eye on your father, if that's what you're worried about."

I tried to toss it off. "That old rummy? I don't care if he drinks himself into an early grave."

He tapped my cheek. "Your tongue wags too much." He poked my chest. "What's your heart saying?"

"That I'd better not leave either of you alone." I left him with a warning to be careful and his cheerful promise to ignore my advice. I'll never know how he'd managed to live this long sticking his nose in other people's business the way he did.

By then, the sidewalks were emptying of bystanders, but a few kids were picking up the stray pennies and nickels. Seeing them scramble for small change made me feel sad. Was I any better? I'd probably wind up like my old man and that scared me.

I was thinking such dark thoughts that I wasn't paying any attention and bumped into someone. It was a Guest as ancient as Grandpa Joe.

"Well," he asked in Chinese, "aren't you going to apologize?"

It had been as much his fault as it was mine, so I didn't see any reason to. And I was feeling fed-up with Chinatown and its ways, so I knew just how to get his goat. "I don't know what you're saying," I said in English.

He scowled at me. "You shame yourself," he ranted in broken English. "You Chinese."

"I'm an American," I mocked him. "I was born here. China's got nothing to do with me."

Well, that really set him off. "You're no better than your father. You'll die in an alley just like he will." He ranted on and on.

Except for Grandpa Joe and another old-timer, Uncle Quail, all the Guests did was scold me because I didn't act like some snot-nose immigrant who didn't even know not to cross on a red light. They'd find fault with me for everything, from the way I stood and walked to that I chewed gum—look like a cow, they'd complain—and the fact I drank soda—bad for your stomach.

They acted like I was the foreigner when they were. They might live most of their lives in America, but they thought of themselves as only Chinese and counted the days until they could retire back there.

When Guests picked on me, it was just an excuse to wander on about the good old days that never existed. And they always got around to contrasting me to the way they acted at my age—and I bet they never had been so goody-goody except in another part of their lousy memories.

I put on a burst of speed and left him behind. Still, he tried to follow me, trying to cross on a red light and getting honked at. He alternated between cursing the driver and me.

Suddenly I needed to talk to a friendly face—and there were only a few other people in Chinatown besides Grandpa Joe and Barney who didn't think I was a bum—so I headed over to the fish store to see one of them. Next to Barney, Jean was my best pal. I could hang out with her, talk with her, and she was game for anything, even walking the length of the Golden Gate Bridge when it opened a couple of years ago.

And I could always count on her to understand why we couldn't spend a lot when we went to the Exposition while it was still open. The city had been celebrating the opening of the Golden Gate Bridge and had even built an island out on the bay for an Exposition. It was a fun place to go even when you had no dough, and even more fun when you had some money in your pocket. If the Exposition didn't open next year, Pan Am was going to take it over for their flying boats, the China Clippers. But I hoped they kept reopening the Exposition each year.

Even if I hadn't seen the shade up on the window, I would have known they had a shipment of shrimp in. Jean was in the back of the smelly shop shelling and then deveining the shrimp. She got two bits for every pound, but it took a lot of shelled shrimp to make up that amount. Some singer was warbling "We're in the Money" from the radio in the back, but it wasn't cheering her up at all.

"I hate shrimp," she said.

"When are you going to be done?" I asked. "We could go to the Exposition."

She looked around the room. It was full of baskets of shrimp waiting to be deveined. "I'm going to be here all night. You'd better go on without me."

"I got nothing else to do," I said, pulling up a stool.

Jean slit open the back of a shrimp efficiently and then used the knife tip to yank out the black "vein"— actually the guts of the shrimp.

"I hear Betty's not doing anything either," she teased.

I could feel the blood warming up my cheeks. "Aw, that's done."

"She's still sweet on you," Jean said.

I stuffed my hands in my pockets. "But not her ma." I tried to laugh it off, but the memory still cut sharp as Jean's knife. "In fact, the last time, she chased me off with a cleaver."

"Swords didn't keep Romeo away from Juliet," Jean said.

"Betty's no Juliet," I said. "And anyway, you know I don't get serious about any girl."

"Ain't that the truth," Jean muttered.

"A girl's got to have a mom like yours," I grinned. "Yours is too tired from work to chase me away."

Jean gave me a thin, prim smile. "I typed up some résumés on the store's typewriter. I did them when the storekeeper was gone. They're in my coat." She nodded to it on a hook by the doorway. "I marked up the want ads too."

I hesitated and then asked, "Outside of Chinatown?"

"Where else?" she challenged me. "You know there aren't any jobs in Chinatown. Cutting up shrimp is all I can get."

Even though I'd been competing with whites outside of Chinatown in our basketball hustle, that was only for a short time. Going up against other whites for a job was a whole different matter. I think that's why I'd only tried Chinatown before this.

"I don't know," I said. "I got another iron in the fire, you know. I . . . um . . . got an offer to play basketball."

Jean looked skeptical. "Where?"

So I told her all about Coughlan and Topper while she went on peeling shrimp.

When I was done, she glanced up at me. "So how long will you be gone?"

"I don't know. Months maybe." I shrugged.

"Don't give up looking for a job," Jean urged.

"There are a hundred white guys for every job," I said. "What luck has a Chinese got?"

Jean glanced up from the shrimp. "Plenty, if they're you."

"The Americans even have a saying about it being hopeless, you know. Ever hear of Chinaman's chance?" I asked.

Jean tossed the deveined shrimp into another bucket. "I'll make you a deal. I'll try if you'll try."

"Don't you ever give up?" I asked, exasperated.

"I never quit," she said.

I gave in. "Okay."

She rewarded me with the grin that I liked so much. "Good boy. I marked up some jobs in the want ads." She nodded to a small package. "You'll find one of my father's old shirts and a tie. I'll loan those to you for tomorrow. Now whatever you do, don't lose your temper. Sometimes you're your own worst enemy." She was a regular old lady as she coached me on what to do.

It was nice to have someone in my corner. I stuck out my hand. "Then it's a deal."

Jean, though, kept her hands in her lap. "My hands stink."

I took her hand anyway and shook it. "You're a real pal, Jean."

She gave me an odd, twisted little smile. "I guess I'm glad you think of me that way."

CHAPTER | III

I was going to make good and show all those Guests in Chinatown who said I'd come to no good, so I was up early in the store.

Jean had even starched the shirt, so I decided to do it right by making sure my shoes were shined too and putting on the tie with my suit.

My old man opened a bleary eye. "There's only one reason you'd put on that monkey suit. But you already tried to find a job in Chinatown. There's nothing."

I found my résumés. "This time I'm trying outside of Chinatown."

He sat up as he began to guffaw. "Where do you get these crazy ideas? No one's going to hire you." His laugh ended in the dry rattle of a cough.

"That attitude's why you've been a drunk all your life,"

I said. I got him a glass of water, which he treated like poison but drank anyway.

Then I checked my reflection on the glass of the beer company wall clock. "But I'm going places."

"You'll see," my old man jeered. "They'll kick you in the teeth just like they did me."

I strode out of the store. I'd show him. I'd show all of Chinatown. I'd give Jean and Grandpa Joe and Uncle Quail a reason to believe in me.

Jean had been thorough and marked down a dozen jobs and typed up that many résumés.

There wasn't a mistake on any of them either. She'd make a crackerjack secretary—if anyone would hire her. I wondered if she'd be stuck gutting shrimp all her life.

Even though I got to the office a half hour early, there were eight other guys already lined up. A pile of application forms were on a chair, weighted down with a rock, so I took one. I'd made sure to bring the fountain pen that Grandpa Joe had given me as a graduation present, but other guys were filling out their forms in pencil.

There was everyone ranging from a nervous kid who didn't look like he was out of junior high to a potbellied, middle-aged man. Some were in suits; some looked like they had slept in their clothes.

It took a while to fill out the form because you had to write a short essay on what you could do for the company. By the time I finished, there were over fifty of us and more climbing the stairs all the time, and by the time the office opened, the line snaked down the stairs to the street and the application forms had run out.

We filed in one by one for the interview and when it was my turn, I found myself face-to-face with a balding, owlish-looking man in a bow tie. He looked at my transcript and then at my application form. Then he looked up at me. "Well, son, I saw over a hundred applicants yesterday and so far you're the most impressive. It's not just your grades, but this little essay you wrote was the best. You're smart. You can express yourself."

I grinned. "Thanks." I figured the job was as good as mine.

"Heck, with your qualifications, you ought to be training for my job. But," the interviewer said ominously, "I can't hire a Chinese when there are white men without jobs."

"You just said I was the best man, though," I protested.

"The best *yellow* man," he corrected me.

My temper exploded in me like a flash of lightning . . . just like my nickname. I almost hit him, but Grandpa Joe had always told me to count to ten and then count to ten again. And whenever I didn't remember, I got in trouble.

Slowly I unclenched my fists and gritted my teeth. Jean had coached me on what to say. "Keep it in your files. Maybe some other job will come up," I said.

"Try some other place, son," the manager said, and slid it back to me.

I took it numbly. Outside his office, I thought all the Americans there were smirking at me.

In the back of my mind, I could hear my old man laughing and sneering, "I told you so."

I wanted to quit trying then and there, but I'd made a promise to Jean, and you don't break your word to a pal.

So I worked my way down the list of jobs at the other offices and stores. There were the same lines everywhere I went and the same answer for me: How can they hire a Chinese when whites don't have jobs?

So I swallowed my pride. Okay, so I wouldn't be at a desk. It would be okay to sweat for a few years. I went all over San Francisco—to the warehouses and even down to Butchertown. But it was always the same result.

I kept plugging away anyway, even though the starch went out of my shirt and I felt as hot and tired and sweaty as if I'd played a dozen games.

I didn't think it could get much worse until I went to a junkyard where the owner just crumpled up my application form and laughed at the ridiculousness of a Chinese even thinking of working for him.

I felt like the biggest loser. I was supposed to be the smart one. Why had I ever let Jean set me up like this? Jean might have brains, but she didn't know about the real world. She'd bought our teachers' con: Work hard and you'll get ahead.

No, it was my old man who was right: It's a sucker's game.

Back on the sidewalk again, I tore up the newspaper and the last résumé and dumped them into a trash can. I'd kept my word to her. I didn't have to try anymore.

I thought I'd better save the carfare, so I walked home. It seemed like every block had a couple of people selling apples for a nickel apiece. And there were more people begging, including legless veterans from the war.

And if America treated Americans that way, what chance did a Chinese have? In the distance, I could see the Bay Bridge, which had opened three years ago. It cut off the bottom of the sky like a ruler.

For a brief moment, I thought how easy it would be to just drop from it into the bay. But then I laughed at myself. Outside of Chinatown, no one cared if there was one less Chinese or not, and in Chinatown, the Guests would just nod their heads because a bad end was always what they had predicted for me.

Well, I'd go on living just to spite them. I glanced at a clock in a store.

It was six by the time I got back to the grocery store. Uncle Quail was there. He'd probably come up from Concepcion near Santa Cruz with a basket of his dried, salted sand dabs. The hem of his coat was as ragged as ever—just like a quail's tail, which is how he got his nickname. And he smelled of fish.

Uncle Quail had sort of adopted me, so he was like a second father. Grandpa Joe had said he'd lost his family in the wars that had gone on in China in the twenties when warlords and bandits were cutting up the country. He'd never been able to make enough to let him go back to China anyway, even if the Japanese weren't there. He made it clear I could have stayed with him, but he could barely feed himself—let alone a growing boy. So I couldn't do that to him.

"Cal-l-vin," he greeted me. His tongue always had a little trouble with *l*'s, so he always took care to enunciate them. "You look thin."

So did he, but I minded my manners. "I've been busy."

"You come down to see me sometime again," he said. "I'll fatten you up while you watch the sea otters."

I'd liked the sea otters when I was a kid. His little cove had been my haven. It would have been so nice to have hid there, but then Ah Lee snapped me back to reality. He'd let us live in his storeroom in exchange for keeping his business's books. "Your old man's already potted."

Even after hearing it all my life, it still hurt a little, but I tried to pass it off with a shrug. "So what else is new?"

Ah Lee pried open the till to pay Uncle Quail. "I pay him to balance the books."

"Then don't let him take out his salary in liquor," I said.

He glared at me. "It's not your place to tell me or your old man what to do."

I don't know why I still tried to protect my old man. "I know your scam. You give my old man small change for a salary and then charge him retail for the liquor he buys."

Ah Lee made a disgusted noise. "Native-born have no brains."

Normally I wouldn't say anything. The storeroom was dry even if it was cramped. However, I'd taken enough lumps for one day.

"Oh, I got brains," I said. "Everyone's got a game going. The smart ones like me know they're playing in one. The dumb ones, like you, don't. Instead, you call it tradition and law."

Ah Lee began the Lecture. "China has been around for more than four thousand years."

I jerked my thumb at my chest. "And all that time they've been playing people like my old man for chumps. But not me."

I saw the same contemptuous look in Ah Lee's eyes that I saw in the eyes of all the Chinatowners. "Well, Mr. Smarty-Pants. Either you get the books balanced, or you and the old rummy are outside on your cans."

And I knew he had me. As miserable a life as we led in his storeroom, there would be hundreds of jobless who would be glad to get it. It had been bad enough having to beg for a job all day, but now I had to come back and crawl before this toad.

As I stood there helplessly clenching my fists, Ah Lee gave a triumphant grunt and turned on his radio, tuning in to some comedy show. As the laughter poured from the set, I heard a truck horn honk outside.

Uncle Quail plucked at my sleeve. "That's Ah Po. Cal-l-vin, you come with me. We can ride back in his truck together."

I guess I'd gotten Barney's bug, because I never wanted to get out of town more than right then. But I heard a noise in the storeroom. It would have served my old man right if I'd dumped him, but then he'd wind up in the gutter for sure. And there was something in me that couldn't let that happen. "Thanks. Maybe some other time."

The light was on in the storeroom. The old man was sitting on a crate with a half-empty bottle on his knee. "I just can't get the books to balance," he said, staring at the pages hopelessly. Another crate served as a desk with a ledger and an abacus.

I knelt by the improvised desk. "Can you even see the pages anymore?"

He smirked almost proudly. "No." He nodded his head to an open can of sardines and a half loaf of bread. "Dinner?" The motion left him a little wobbly, like a broken metronome.

I slipped a sardine out of the can and slapped it on

a piece of bread. "Thanks." As I munched, I tried to straighten out the mess. His notes were little more than scrawls by now.

"So did you get anywhere dressing up like a peacock?" He took another swig from the bottle. The liquor used up what little salary he got from the storekeeper. I didn't answer, but my face said it all. His lips curled up mockingly. "So how many doors got slammed in your face?"

"At least I tried," I snapped. I began to check the receipts against the ledger. I liked numbers almost as much as I liked basketball. Numbers didn't change. They didn't lie. And when you found hidden patterns, it was like learning a secret magic that no one else knew.

"You know what Americans mean when they say 'Chinaman's Chance'?" he sneered. "It means you got no hope at all."

In school, all my American teachers had assumed that the parents of every Chinese kid made them study and work hard. But something had poisoned that dream in my old man. All that was left was sour grapes—and the need to tear down anyone who was trying to get ahead. Anything I got, I got on my own. Well, that was a joke because I didn't have anything more than my old man.

I let him spew out more bile while I did his job. He just kept drinking steadily, listening to the dripping toilet in one corner of the room. By the time I had found the mistake, he had finished the bottle.

"There. It's all balanced," I said, slamming the ledger shut and getting up. We'd have a roof over our heads for one more night.

He held out his hand. "I need money, Mr. High-and-Mighty."

If I still had the ten bucks, I wouldn't have given him any of it. "You'll just waste it on booze."

"Liar." He rose unsteadily to his feet. "I sacrificed for you. Now it's your turn to help me," he said.

"What sacrifice? Every time I try to climb up the ladder, you pull me back into the gutter," I said. *Maybe if I'd had a real father, I might've gotten some breaks in life.*

He began to take off his belt. "I'll teach you to behave."

I tried to work things out with him. "If I leave, who's going to balance the books for you?"

"You respect me," he said, and swung the belt.

His aim wasn't too good, and I jumped to the side so that most of the blow caught a crate.

For a moment, I thought about hitting him. I was a head taller than him and in a lot better shape. But I just couldn't. Call me a chump too. Even so, I couldn't let him get away with this.

"Give me something to respect instead of a drunken old fool," I said.

"Respect me," he demanded.

The next swing was faster and more accurate. It was harder too. It hurt.

Still I couldn't fight back, but this time when he swung, I grabbed the belt itself. My palm stung, but I held on. "This is why I hate you," I said.

"Respect me," the old man said, trying to pull the belt free.

For a minute, we played tug-of-war, but the old man was drunk and out of shape. When I yanked the belt out of his hands, he fell backward into a pile of boxes.

He just lay there, wriggling his arms and legs like an overturned turtle. "Respect me, respect me," he whimpered, beginning to cry.

The anger was red hot inside me, and for a moment I felt like giving him a taste of his own belt; but then I took a long hard stare at him—the red nose, the watery eyes, the sagging face and body. Disgusted, I tossed the belt on top of him. "Go drown yourself in a bottle."

He raised a palm. "Then give me money," he begged. "Please, please."

The bottle had even taken away his pride now. "Here," I said and, taking off my shoe, I took out my last dollar and threw it at him. Then I left.

Uncle Quail was gone with Ah Po by then, but Ah Lee was sitting down on a stool, frowning as usual, despite the best efforts of the comedian on the radio. It was as if hearing people happy only made him unhappier. Yet in all the time we'd lived there, I'd never heard him listen to anything else but comedy shows and always with the same miserable expression.

"I heard the noise," he said. "If you broke anything, you're paying."

"Take it out of that small change you call a salary," I snapped.

Ah Lee saw the red welt on my arm. "If he'd given you more of the belt, you wouldn't be so wild now." He threw a scrap of paper at me. "A girl named Jean called. She said to call her at the fish store."

I snatched the paper up from the floor, but I couldn't read the note. "Why didn't you tell me when I came in?"

"I forgot. Anyway, I'm not your secretary," he said and pointed to the wall. "And use the pay phone to call her."

But I didn't want to talk to Jean. I didn't ever want to talk to her. I didn't ever want to see her. I just wanted to get out of there.

I was desperate enough to try anything. I might be gutter trash to the rest of the world, but on a basketball court, I was king. If I had to leave San Francisco to play, then that's what I'd do.

So I grabbed my gym shoes and headed out the door.

CHAPTER | IV

I t was funny to head through Japantown. The Japanese were shopping in the brightly lit stores for supper or shoveling food into their faces just like the Chinese did in Chinatown.

What made me laugh were the souvenir stores. In the windows Chinese silk dresses hung side by side with Japanese kimonos. It was the same way in the Chinatown shops. No matter how patriotic a shopkeeper was, a buck was a buck.

Here and there some loyal Japanese had put up a picture of the emperor. I knew a bunch of kids in Japantown because I'd played in gyms and playgrounds against them. And they didn't care about Japan any more than I did about China. That was the country where their folks were born, but it had nothing to do with them. We didn't have any quarrel with one another—except maybe when we got onto a basketball court. But I never knew when I'd run across some patriotic numskull who was the Japantown equivalent of Zack Jeh—or some recent immigrant from Japan—who'd decide to fight out the war here and now with me, so I started to jog.

When I trotted into the gym and heard the squeak of rubber soles on polished floorboards and sniffed the familiar smells, I knew I was home.

Topper looked annoyed when he saw me. "You're late," he frowned.

The others were holding a shootaround. Barney was standing there like he was supposed to be part of it, but as I headed toward them, I noticed that no one was passing to him.

The others looked as ancient as Topper and Jack, and one of them even had a mustache—a natty little number like the kind Clark Gable sported—and his hair was slicked back with pomade.

"This is Calvin Chin," Topper said.

"I saw you play in a gym once," a beefy guy in a bright aloha shirt said to me. "You're not bad for . . . a twerp." He introduced himself as Alphonse and shook my hand with a grip like a vise. "I'm a forward, but I can fill in for the center. Be nice to me because I get the rebounds for you guards."

"Watch out for this guy," a big guy with glasses warned. "He's a real joker." He held out his hand. "Name's

Longfellow—no jokes about the height either. My mom liked his poetry." He was the team's center.

The guy with the mustache clapped a hand on his shoulder. "But we call him the Professor 'cause he's always got his nose buried in a book. But in a game, he's got a hook shot no one can stop. I'm Hollywood." He turned so I could admire his profile. "I play the other forward and spell Tops at guard when he starts wheezing."

"You're the one who gets tired from the late hours," Topper shot back.

"You always dress up for all your practices?" the Professor asked me, amused. I hadn't changed from the suit I had worn for the interview.

"You've got to have style," I said. I took off my coat and tie and rolled up my sleeves. Then, as I changed into my gym shoes, Topper filled me in on their strategy. Because all of our opponents were going to be taller than us, we'd have to count on our speed and smarts. On offense, we'd take shots from long range and then use our speed and smarts to get the rebound so we could take a shot close in.

On defense, we'd always have to be in the right position to cut off drives to the basket, anticipate our opponents' passes and then intercept them, and steal the ball whenever we could. That would set up a fast break, and it was up to me and Topper to knife to the basket before the other team could set up its own defense. And sharp ballhandling and quick passing could create other opportunities against bigger but slower foes if they tried to press us.

The plan was obvious because it was similar to the one Barney and I used in our con. "I'm not stupid," I snapped as I laced up my shoes.

Topper gave a grunt. "Think you know everything, don't you? Listen, wise guy. There's going to be hecklers in every game we play. Think you can handle it without punching half the town?"

"If you pay me enough," I snapped.

They started showing me some of their plays with Topper standing off to the side as the coach. They did everything on the run and even then Topper wasn't satisfied because he kept shouting, "Push it up!"

And when they got under the basket, they moved the ball around a lot. Our bigger, slower opponents were bound to make mistakes as they tried to keep shifting to the man who had the ball.

Topper's team worked together smoothly, like cogs in an oiled machine, but Barney and I weren't familiar with the plays, so we got the brunt of Topper's scolding. And I found myself resenting him for trying to make us into little robots. Who was he to call the shots?

He could read my thoughts off my face and he grunted, "How long has it been since you've played on a real team?"

"I've played in tournaments plenty of times," I said defensively.

He gave a snort. "Yeah, I've seen you. You played like it was only you and Barney while the three other guys were just there to hand you a towel. But you're not getting away with that here."

Barney's role was simple. He set picks. They could have substituted a statue on wheels. Mine was just as easy too. I was under tight instructions not to take any shots under any circumstances. I was just supposed to be an errand boy who had to bring the ball up and then toss it to them so they could hog all the glory. For all the skill it required, they could have replaced me with a roller skate and set the ball on it and then sent it wheeling along.

And to be honest, I couldn't even do that well today. The trouble was, I'd run over the hills to get there so I was a little slow and tired, so Topper was on me from the start.

"Is that all you got?" Topper demanded. "Come on! Push it up! Are you part turtle?"

I wasn't about to tell him the truth and give the team a chance to rib me. "I got plenty when I'm not bored."

But it was such basic stuff that I couldn't help yawning—when I suddenly felt something sting me. "Ow," I said, giving a jump. The ball hit my foot and rolled out of bounds.

The others started to laugh. The only one who wasn't grinning was Topper. He had a slingshot. "Bring it up fast."

By the time I got the ball, he had his slingshot loaded again. "Okay, okay," I said, starting to run.

And the Little Hitler kept shouting at me over a lot of little stuff. "Didn't you see Alphonse? He was open under the basket."

At first, I tried to reason with him. "But I had my shot."

Topper frowned. "You shoot from there, and maybe you hit it how many times?"

"Three out of five?"

Topper jabbed a finger toward Alphonse. "But Alphonse can hit it seven out of ten from his spot."

Finally Topper tore at his hair, twisting it into spikes. "No, no, no."

I stopped, getting ready to duck if he took out his slingshot. "What's the matter now? I was running."

"Don't get fancy with the dribble. Get the ball up-court."

I slammed the basketball down so hard, it almost bounced back up to the ceiling. "This isn't basketball."

Topper waved his hand at the others. "In case you haven't noticed, basketball is a team sport."

Which is what every coach had said to me. They didn't understand anything. So I said what I always did when they started to nag me. "I quit."

"Is that what you are? A quitter?" Topper threw the ball hard at me. Out of sheer self-protection, I raised my hands and caught it. However, the force of the throw felt like getting hit in the stomach with a rock.

"Oof." The air rushed out of me, and when I finally managed to straighten, I panted, "You can't make me play."

Topper just reached a hand into his jacket pocket. "The last few times, it was beans. But I got pebbles too. Those won't just sting. They'll leave bruises."

I thought of that office manager and then I thought of my old man. Without basketball, I was a nothing.

"Just do it his way for now, Cal," Barney whispered.

"Okay, okay," I said, starting to dribble forward again. As I moved, though, I felt a little twinge from the bruise on my behind. I'd find a way to pay back Topper somehow.

After a while, even Topper had to give me my due. "I thought you'd be raw on some skills, but somebody coached you in good fundamentals."

I guess my high school coach might have been a jerk when it came to race, but he'd drummed the basics into me.

Topper's partner, Coughlan, had been watching us with a silent intensity all this time. Suddenly he shaped a T with his fingers. "Time!" he called.

However, as I headed toward the bench to rest my sore muscles, he gripped my shoulder and steered me toward a corner of the gym where the others couldn't hear us. "Let's you and me have a little chat, Flash."

"My name's Calvin," I said. "Flash is a tag other people gave me."

"You listen to me and you'll be Flash for real." He winked. "You could be the biggest thing since fried rice."

Well, why did I want to be Calvin? Calvin was just garbage, so it'd be nice to become someone else. As much as I wanted that, though, I knew when someone was trying to pull a fast one. "Whether you call it fried rice or fertilizer, I know what you're trying to sell me."

"Call me Jack." Coughlan cleared his throat as he dropped his hand. "You remind me a little of myself at your age," he said. He'd lost his smirk and looked serious for once. "Talent as huge as the chip on my shoulder—heck, it was more like a whole tree than a chip. But it felt a lot easier to carry when I got my share of the spotlight. A few years ago, the Celtics' stars were Joe Lapchick, Dutch Dehnert, Nat Holman, and yours truly," he said, and then bent so he could tap his knee, "but then I wrecked this one night. And it was all over." He sighed.

I pantomimed playing a violin. "I think you're gassing me with that sob story."

He didn't get mad though. He just gave me that smirk of his. "Think you're pretty tough, don't you? Well, let me tell you something: There's always someone smarter. And meaner. Ever hear of Hell's Kitchen?"

"No, but from the name it sounds tough," I admitted.

"That's where I grew up in New York, and the guys there would have chewed you up for breakfast and then spit you out," Jack said.

"Yeah, sure," I said skeptically. He said he was one of eight kids in a room that sounded smaller than Jean's place; and if he wasn't getting into a scrap outside, he was getting into one at home with his brothers and sisters—all of whom could use their fists. Dinnertime turned into a real free-for-all with everyone trying to snatch as much of their skimpy meal as he or she could before it was gone.

"When I was small," he said, "I'd go to bed hungry sometimes because I wasn't fast enough, so I learned that if I wanted anything, I had to grab it for myself. So let me give you some advice: You only get one shot at the spotlight. And man, oh, man, it's sweet while you're in it, but it's only yours for a little while."

"So what's so great about the spotlight?" I demanded suspiciously.

He looked serious for once as he waved a hand at the city beyond the gym walls. The spotlight can get you a lot more than newspaper clippings. It can get you everything you've dreamed about. But only if you've got somebody who can steer the spotlight to you. And that guy is me."

I was starting to figure him out. "And by helping me, you help yourself."

He pantomimed turning on a lightbulb. "Bingo. I take care of you, and you take care of me."

I was always suspicious when strangers said they were doing you favors out of the kindness of their sweet, little hearts, but I could understand a deal that benefited the both of us. Maybe things were finally beginning to go my way—but I'd had so many bad breaks that I didn't want to believe there was a glimmer of hope. "I'll see," I said cautiously. "But just tell me one thing: Is it better to be in the spotlight or to own it?"

Jack's smirk snapped back into place. "The game on the court's just part of a bigger game, kid." With a wink he headed back to the rest of the team, spreading his arms in a sweeping motion. "Gather around, guys."

When the team had gathered around him, he picked up a box from a bench and, with a flourish, drew out something sewn from bright scarlet silk. At first, I thought it was a flag, but then I saw it was a uniform jersey with the number I in gold. He turned it around so we could see DRAGONS on the back with a picture of a Chinese dragon curled underneath.

"But we're the All Stars," Topper protested.

"Maybe that name will sell tickets in Frisco, but not in the rest of America," Jack said.

I never wanted to wear anything more than that jersey. And that need surprised me because, ever since I'd gotten kicked off the team, I'd told myself that uniforms were for fools.

It just all hit me suddenly. Remembering how the kids at high school treated athletes, hearing the crowds in a gym, coming out onstage during rallies. Being someone *big* in high school instead of being a zero.

Jack must have seen the hunger in my eyes because he tossed it over to me. "Try it on, kid."

When I pulled it on, I stood for a moment in the gym, imagining the cheers, the band—everything that I'd missed after I was kicked off the team. And more: For the first time in my life I had hope.

Jack nodded. "It looks good on you." He handed out more uniforms with different numbers.

I know it sounds stupid, but the uniform almost made it worthwhile having to put up with Topper bossing me around and being a benchwarmer and errand boy.

"Dragons, I kind of like it," Hollywood said as he held his jersey against his chest.

The others made some nice comments about their new togs, but it wasn't such a big deal to them. And I realized I was behaving like an idiot so I started to take it off.

Jack waved a hand. "Keep it, kid."

Topper frowned. "One's *my* number."

Jack got a sly look that I would come to know well. "Why don't you play a game of twenty-one for it."

Alphonse tossed the ball to Topper, who came right at me with this wicked grin. "Don't dog it, kid. Or do I have to get out the slingshot?"

I'd been feeling plenty tired, but that sneer on his face gave me a shot of adrenaline. I was just so determined to

wipe that smile off his face, off all their faces, the manager, my old man. Everyone.

I crouched on the balls of my feet. I figured he knew
I was faster so he'd try to fake me out. First, he tried to
tempt me by showing me the ball while he dribbled, but I
didn't lunge for it because he was skilled enough to pivot
and dart past me while I was off-balance. Then he tried
some head jerks and leg moves, but I'd learned in the
playgrounds to keep watching the trunk of the body and
when I saw that begin to move left, I knew he was trying
to drive.

And suddenly there was that sweet basketball. It
seemed to move in slow motion as it bounced off the gym
floor. I slapped it away.

I heard Topper swear, but I was already dribbling
away from his desperate grab.

I was grinning from ear to ear after I made my basket.
"Maybe I'm the one who ought to have the slingshot."

"You only pick my pocket once," Topper growled as
he caught my pass.

When he crouched and started to dribble, I licked my
chops and went in for the steal, but he timed it beauti-
ful, waiting for the instant when I reached out before he
pivoted so that my hand touched empty air instead of
the ball. At the same time, he kicked his foot against my
ankle and the next thing I knew I was looking up at the
ceiling. Well, he had warned me.

My legs started to give out after that, and my lungs were burning from the run there. Topper ran rings around me, so he made twenty points before I even had eleven.

"I'll take that," Topper said, holding the Number 1 jersey—my jersey—over his head in victory.

"I'm getting it back," I warned him.

Topper grinned insolently. "Anytime."

Jack whispered to me, "You listen to old Jack and it'll be yours sooner rather than later."

Watching Topper preen with my jersey, I made my pact with the Devil right then and there.

"You got yourself a deal," I grunted.

CHAPTER | V

"Hey," Jean called. Her voice echoed in the gym. I turned to see her. With her was Grandpa Joe and Tiger, Barney's girlfriend. Tiger always dressed a little better than the rest of us. I had assumed that her family was rich because of the way she dressed and because Barney had told me once that they had a jade heirloom, an owl or something. However, Jean had told me Tiger's mother sewed clothes in a sweatshop, so she turned rags and scraps into something nice.

I felt embarrassed that they had seen Topper beat me. "What are you doing here?"

"I thought we could celebrate," Jean said, and waved a steno pad over her head in triumph. "I got a job. I aced the typing and dictation tests. Mainly it'll be filing in an office downtown, but who knows?"

Barney smiled ingratiatingly. "Are you treating?"

I dug into Barney's duffel bag for the towel. "Where's your money?" I said, already suspecting the worst.

Barney shrugged and gave me his usual little-boy-with-his-hand-caught-in-the-cookie-jar look. "I would've sworn that no one could've sunk the six ball in the pocket."

It was just like I thought: After getting his snack, Barney had gotten suckered into a game with some pool sharks. I suppose there was a certain symmetry to his life: What he won with a basketball, he lost with his cue.

"Well, I'm tapped out," I said, slapping my hands against my empty pockets. I didn't tell them that I'd sacrificed most of it for Grandpa Joe, because with my bad-boy reputation they never would have believed it. "You know how money just trickles through my fingers."

Jean asked the question I had been dreading. "How did the job interviews go?"

"I'm going on the road," I said.

Barney clapped a hand on my shoulder. "Cal and I are turning pro."

"I told you," Grandpa Joe said.

"I had to hear it myself," Jean said, and then gave me a disappointed look. "Did you even try the want ads, Calvin?" She always used my formal name when she wanted me to act grown up.

How could I tell her about all the humiliation? "Can you see me sitting in a chair from nine to five?" I tried to joke to cover up the hurt. "I'm an active kind of guy."

"But this sounds like a con to us," Tiger said. "Who'd pay to see grown men play a kids' game? More importantly, who'd pay to see Chinese do it?"

"That's the gimmick," Barney said. "All those yokels out there think we're just laundrymen."

Grandpa Joe threw me a towel from Barney's bag. "I made some inquiries after Flash told me about it." He might have his head in the clouds when it came to his causes, but he wasn't going to let any harm come to his grandson. "I think this is legitimate. This is what you want to do?"

I knew he meant doing it for myself. "What do you think?"

"I think you never looked happier than when you were on this court," he grunted. "But you better let me handle the contracts."

"You've always told me money wasn't important," I said.

He patted me on the shoulder. "Sure, but you boys need to get more out of this than just satisfaction."

Jean hesitated and then squared her shoulders as if she was performing a duty rather than doing something she wanted to. "I'll help you, Mr. Young. These guys can't loaf all their lives."

Grandpa Joe looked relieved. "You've got a much better head for negotiating."

I yanked at her arm. "Jean, what do you think you're doing?"

Jean was suddenly all business, putting on the same expression that made the storekeepers quail all along Grant Avenue. "Just how much are you getting paid any-way, Mr. Chin?"

"Well . . . unh . . ." I looked helplessly at Barney. "What did he say? A hundred?"

Barney scratched his head sheepishly. "I think so."

"You dopes," Tiger sniffed. "You'd play for a can of beans." She elbowed Barney in the ribs. "Make Jean your agent."

"Yeah, I guess," Barney said, rubbing the sore spot. "Why not?" He didn't mind anything so long as he got some fun out of it.

Jean swiveled back to me and said in the same cold tone she used when she was beating down the prices of the butcher, "What about you, Calvin? Do you want to ride the trolley or walk home tonight?"

"I thought you'd loan me the carfare," I wheedled, but my words were about as effective as a popgun against a battleship.

"I'll give an advance to my client," Jean said stiffly. "However, if you absolve all ties with me, you're on your own—and on foot."

Grandpa Joe stuffed his hands into his pockets. "She'll make a better agent than me."

Barney spread his arms. "She can't do any worse than us."

I realized the main thing was to get out of town and get a stake for when I came back. "Okay," I shrugged.

"I'll go with you, but you do the talking." Grandpa Joe nodded to Jean, and they pivoted abruptly and walked over to Topper and Jack.

"We have to speak, Mr. Tom," Jean said.

"Sure, kid, you want an autograph?" Topper asked. He was already reaching for a pen.

"In a way," Jean said. She nodded to Grandpa Joe. "My associate, Mr. Young, and I would like to discuss our clients' contracts."

Jack gave her a puzzled look. "Clients?"

Jean waved a hand behind her to indicate Barney and me. "Laurel and Hardy over there."

Jack glanced over Jean's head at us, and Barney nodded while I shrugged reluctantly.

Satisfied, Jean turned back to Topper and Jack. "Well, Mr.—?"

"Jack Coughlan," Jack said.

"Late of the New York Celtics," Topper said. "And I'm Topper Tom."

"Yes, I know who you are, Mr. Tom. You've left a trail of broken hearts all through Chinatown," Jean said so icily it could have kept an icebox cold for a month. "Shall we move over to a corner with Mr. Young?"

The rest of the team drifted by. A couple of them had girlfriends. Now that we'd proved ourselves in the game, they were willing to introduce their dates and talk to us.

I left it to Barney to chat with them as I watched Grandpa Joe and Jean anxiously. Jack no longer looked amused. In fact, his face had grown red and stormy. "She's going to get us thrown off the team." I tried to pull free from Tiger's grip. "I've got to stop her."

Tiger held on to me for dear life. "Give me a hand, Barney."

"Well, I . . ." Barney said, hesitating.

"Or I go home with Jean without you," Tiger warned. "I hope you like smooching with Flash because he'll be the only one with you tonight."

I had managed to yank my arm free, but Barney got me in a sleeper hold. "Sorry, Flash. You made a promise to Jean."

I knew better than to wrestle with Barney. He'd always won those matches ever since we were small. I could only stand there helplessly and watch while I got tossed off a team again.

Finally, a frowning Jack and Topper shook her hand. Then, on her steno pad, she wrote something down—I guess it was the terms of our contract. Grandpa Joe and Jack signed it and Topper witnessed it.

Clutching it against her stomach as if it were a crown, Jean came over to us with Grandpa Joe. "You and Flash just have to sign this," she said to Barney. "Grandpa Joe is your legal guardian." She turned to me. "What about your dad?"

I shrugged. "Grandpa Joe can represent me too—if I like the contract."

Barney gave me a playful shake. "Come on. Be a good boy."

"I want to read it first," I said sullenly.

"Can't," Jean said as she held it out with a pen. "It's in shorthand."

"Then read it to me," I said.

Jean pretended to pout. "Cal, don't you trust me?"

A sap like Barney was all too happy to sign his life away. "How much did you finally get for us?" That was the all-important question anyway.

"I'm not going to tell you," Jean said, holding it out to me.

"But it's our money," I protested.

"Which you will spend the first chance you get and then have nothing to show for the trip," Jean said. "Let's just say you're going to get what the rest of the veterans are getting."

I shot a dark look at Jack and Topper. It was a shock to hear that the average salary was even more than a hundred.

"Mr. Coughlan will wire me the bulk of your salary each week," Grandpa Joe explained, "and I'll deposit it into two bank accounts that I'll open for you." He shook his head. "When I talked you boys into coming to the Chinatown Y to learn the game, I never thought you could make a career out of it."

Barney was shocked. "But we've got to have some dough when we're on the road."

"Jack will give you part of your wages," Jean said. She held her forefinger and thumb almost touching each other. "I might say, a minuscule portion." She smiled pleasantly. "If you're careful with your spending, you'll have enough to amuse yourselves but not enough to get you into real trouble."

"Give that back," Barney said, trying to take the steno pad. "I changed my mind."

Tiger shoved him away from her friend. "Jean's right. Don't worry, baby. I'll keep the books. Everything will be on the up and up."

Jean held out the steno pad to me. "You next, Cal."

"You're crazy," I snapped. "There's no way I'll agree to that."

Jean leaned in close. "Even if you manage to hold on to your money, your dad will talk you into handing it over to him."

She knew my dad almost as well as I did. "You'll take care of him?"

Grandpa Joe nodded. "He's not going to go hungry."

"Just a little thirsty," I said. Grandpa Joe and Jean were probably going to put him on the wagon whether he liked it or not. Real pals are the ones who get you to do the right things even when you don't want to. Well, my old man had it coming. "Okay."

Jack and Topper passed as I was signing the contract. "You'd better find out what her percentage is," Jack said, amused. "She drives a hard bargain."

"Hey, Mr. Coughlan," Barney coaxed, "what about an advance?"

Grandpa Joe rapped his head with a knuckle. "That's why we're going to handle your money, knucklehead. Forget it."

Jack pivoted and walked backward a few steps while he spread his hands. "You're on your own, Barney."

"Just remember the 'water' clause," Grandpa Joe reminded him.

"I can bring the tea to them, but I can't make them drink it," Jack warned.

"They will," Grandpa Joe said, eyeing Barney and then me.

Barney groaned. "Not the railroad story again."

"And the coal mines," Grandpa Joe said and launched into his standard lecture. "Hot tea was what kept the Chinese healthy. They didn't drink the water."

"Yeah, yeah," Barney grunted, rolling his eyes.

Grandpa Joe made a show of yawning. "Well, it's past my bedtime. I'm going home."

Barney hugged his grandfather affectionately. "Don't give us that baloney. You'll go home and work on stuff like you always do."

"I have to keep busy." Grandpa Joe shrugged and motioned for me to walk with him. When we were out of Barney's earshot, he leaned in and whispered, "Take care of my grandson, Calvin. I love him, but God bless him, he's got more heart than sense."

I loved this old man, so it was easy to make the promise. "Sure," I grinned. "You practically raised me with Barney, so that makes him sort of my brother."

Grandpa Joe patted me on the shoulder. "I knew I could count on you."

When I went back, I handed the steno pad to Jean. "Hey, just what is your percentage anyway?"

"You're going to hate it," she warned.

I got ready for her to take a big bite, but I thought of all the favors she had done for me in the past besides tonight. I guess she had earned it.

"What is it?"

"Barney's going to have to write Tiger, and you're going to have to write me," Jean said, and pointed to a line of squiggles on the page.

"Will postcards count?" Barney asked hopefully.

"I want more than 'Having a good time. Wish you were here,'" Tiger said.

"We'll share them with Grandpa Joe," Jean promised.

Barney never stopped to think. That was his trouble. "Sure," he said breezily and took her arm. "Now where are we going tonight? So how's about you loan us the denaro.

You know we're good for it. How's about we catch that new Judy Garland flick you've been wanting to see? *The Wizard of Ooze*, wasn't it?"

Tiger sighed, dusted off her purse as if there were cobwebs on it from lack of use, and snapped it open. "I guess that's the only way I'm going to get to see it."

Jean set her hands against our backs and steered us toward the door. "The boys are heading straight home. They're in training now, Tiger."

She was taking this agent stuff way too seriously.

CHAPTER | VI

I didn't realize how serious until Jean rousted me out of bed at seven the next morning.

"I'm still sore," I groaned. The old man was still sleeping off another bender, so I knew we wouldn't wake him.

"You're in training, big boy." Jean plucked the stale doughnut from my hand. "Tiger's got Barney at the playground."

I made a face. "You're fired."

"And I refuse to be fired," Jean said. "Now get dressed. We got a month to get you in some sort of shape."

"You're enjoying bossing me around way too much," I groused.

"You're such a baby," she said, batting me over the head with the doughnut.

"Ow," I complained. "Don't bruise the merchandise."

❊ ❊ ❊

Our days were busy with training and our evenings with practice. We ate our meals at Tiger's, which sounded great when we first heard the invitation.

Tiger and her four little brothers and sisters lived with their mother in this tiny one-bedroom apartment with just one toilet for the entire floor. Since there always seemed to be some other friends around, the place was a regular madhouse.

It didn't seem to bother Tiger's mother, though. There were times when dinner was a big pot of jook, which is a kind of porridge made from rice and whatever vegetables and meat or fish were in the house. It could be stretched to feed extra freeloaders simply by adding more water— and it usually was. But then Tiger and her mom would fry up a batch of Chinese crullers to dip into the jook. They weren't sugary at all and tasted so good when they came hot from the oil.

So my mouth was watering at the smell of the crullers sizzling in the oil when Tiger plopped a plate of celery before Barney and me. I stared at it suspiciously. "What's this for?"

Tiger leaned a fist on the table. "Why do you think I invited you? Jean and me are going to make sure our clients eat right." Barney opened his mouth to protest and nearly gagged when his girlfriend jammed a celery stalk down his throat. "And no arguments, or we eighty-six you from the apartment permanently."

"All the more for us," Phil piped up. He was Tiger's brother, and I think he was a little jealous of Barney.

So while the others got to eat crullers to their hearts' content, we had to make do with jook and celery.

All the meals went that way. Nothing fatty. Nothing sugary. Tiger's mother felt so sorry for us that she tried to slip us some cookies and got a scolding from both girls. Even a few days later at Halloween it was just apples— and they kept us under strict curfew. There were also all these great movies playing like *Gone with the Wind*, which I would have seen for the special effects, but they told us not to waste money.

They weren't agents. They were prison wardens. It would be a relief to go on the road and get away from them.

Jack started taking a hand during our practices too, and though he couldn't run on his gimpy leg, he could grab rebounds and start us on our fast breaks. He had a pretty good set of hands—"soft" ones that snatched a ball easily from the air as if it had been a feather, and he had tips he'd learned playing from the Celtics like Lapchick, the center. "You don't have to use your whole arm for the tap on the jump ball," he said to the Professor. "Just extend your arm and twist your hand from the wrist. It's quicker and more efficient." When that wound up making the Professor even faster, Jack went up a peg in our estimation.

The team already had some hand signals for plays, but he gave us even more—like ones for where we ought to be when the ball was tapped. We were going to need better communication against some of our opponents, but it meant we had to study after practice. I agreed with Barney when he groaned, "I thought I was done with homework when I finished high school."

The thing I had to work on the most was my defense. Though I'd played for teams in Chinatown tournaments, that had only been temporary. I'd been brought in to make baskets, not prevent them. I hadn't been on an actual team since high school, and defense was really a team effort. Oh, I could play fine one-on-one, but defense required knowing when to switch from my man to another and knowing where I was supposed to be and what my responsibilities were in a particular defensive scheme. And zone defenses, where each of us was responsible for an area, were new to me. It was a whole new level of skills. Some days I felt like I was back in high school cramming for a calculus exam.

I got some extra tutoring from Alphonse, who was the best guy on defense. When he was defending, he'd go into his horse stance from kung fu—looking just like he was riding a horse. He said he had better balance that way, but I never got the hang of that.

It was hard to say who was the better actor, him or Hollywood, at drawing a charging foul. All you had to do was brush Hollywood on your way to the basket and he would be flopping down on the hardwood as if you had rammed him with a truck. On the other hand, Alphonse would stagger back and ham it up as if you had just broken his ribs.

Topper drove us hard, but he didn't get out the slingshot again. He didn't have to. When I got on the court with him, all I could think about was showing I was Number 1. As I got back a little of my legs and wind, he realized he was going to have to push himself to match me—whether it was in strengthening drills or intrasquad games, I always tried to beat him. When he had the ball, I especially liked to stay on him as tight as flypaper. And when I had the ball, I pulled every trick I knew to get past him. I had to admit, though, that he was pretty good for an old guy.

And after practice, there was "special" instruction from Jack. He was serious about being my tutor, and I put up with it in the hopes that I could beat Topper. At first, Jack went over the basic mechanics, but then he began giving me some of the tips he'd picked up as a pro. Among other things, he had me work on taking shots from my left—since I was right-handed, I naturally moved to that side. After a while, I got comfortable taking a shot from either side.

It wasn't long before Barney came to watch and then joined in—and then so did Alphonse, Hollywood, and the Professor because some of what Jack was showing me was new to them as well. Only Topper stayed away—not because he was above using Jack's tips, but because he thought of Jack as a business partner and not a coach. It finally dawned on me that this was also one of Jack's bigger games, because he really was trying to switch the team's loyalty from Topper to me, and by doing that, indirectly to himself.

Before we left San Francisco, Jack had arranged an exhibition game with a team of stiffs called the Gym-Dandies. As I walked toward Kezar Pavilion with Barney, I heard a radio playing through the open window of an apartment. Ted Lewis was on some show, singing about how we were heading for better times. I'd heard a ton of those kind of songs, but they had never seemed to apply to me. However, I was starting to consider the possibilities as we ambled along.

Once we had changed into our uniforms, Jack had some publicity shots taken as the Gym-Dandies warmed up. Topper automatically stood at the center of the team picture as if it was his right, but Jack motioned with his hand. "Calvin, move over by Topper."

The others made room for me, but Topper glared at me like he didn't want to share the spotlight with me. And then Jack took shots of us striking poses. It was all pretty thrilling stuff to Barney and me, and I could see the others were excited too, though they tried to hide it.

But when the photos were done, Topper jerked a thumb at all the team's gear. "Rookies handle that stuff," he said to Barney and me.

I glared at his back as he strolled away.

"Easy, kid," Jack said. "He'll find out who's top dog soon enough. In the meantime"—he handed us a tea-kettle and a can of tea leaves—"these are yours from now on, boys. Boil away."

"On what?" Barney asked.

Jack shrugged. "That's your job." He consulted his memory. "It's Paragraph ten, Clause five, as I recall. You two are to drink tea, not the local water."

"Sure, sure," I said. I took the kettle and can, intending to toss them away the first chance I got.

Jack started to turn away but stopped to look over his shoulder. "And if I don't see your tea, I'm to report back to your agents."

Since they were probably outside, it was too soon to chuck them, but we managed to find a hot plate in an office so we could make tea at least this once.

My stomach did flip-flops when I walked onto the court in my uniform. There were even a couple of reporters and photographers there with flashbulbs popping.

Jack waved his arms grandly. "I want you to meet my boys."

The team members exchanged funny looks with

one another because they didn't like having Jack talk about them as if we were just kids. But I pretended like I hadn't heard.

It was funny watching Topper because he assumed they'd all want to interview him, but they wanted to talk to the Professor. And when they did, it was questions like: "So why's a Singapore Prince playing basketball?"

The Professor opened his mouth but nothing came out. Jack was only too happy to step in. "His Highness was bored, wasn't he?"

And the questions got even more outrageous, like what did the Professor do with his yacht? (Jack: It's in dry dock having the barnacles scraped off.)

Alphonse was a big nightclub crooner in Honolulu whose grandmother had been the former queen of Hawaii. And Jack even had a ukulele, which he whipped out of a paper bag and thrust into Alphonse's startled hands.

All of the questions were based on the biographies Jack had cooked up for us. Among other whoppers, my old man was a politician back in China who had made Chiang Kai-shek and Mao Tse-tung agree to a truce so their armies would fight the Japanese rather than each other.

It was hard to say who had more trouble keeping a straight face during the interview—us or the reporters. I don't think they believed the stories any more than we did, but I guess it made better copy than the truth.

The only one who wasn't enjoying it was Topper, who was ready to blow his stack at being ignored.

When he tried to complain to Jack afterward, Jack just shrugged. "It's the sizzle that's going to draw the crowds in. Then you can wow them, okay?"

The pavilion was where tournaments were played, so it could hold quite a few people, but there were only a few folks in the bleachers that night. Jean, Tiger, Grandpa Joe, and Tiger's mother were there. She was dressed in her best dress, with the jade owl charm around her neck.

I carried in the water bucket for the others and the kettle full of tea for Barney and me. I made a point of holding it up to show them that we were fulfilling our contract.

The game started with me gathering splinters in my behind. Jack sat with me on the bench, looking just as tense and excited as his team.

The pace in the game was a lot different than practice. Though the Dragons were tall for Chinatown, we would be short compared to a lot of American teams. We'd have to compensate for the height difference by running the legs off our opponents.

Right from the start, Topper began shouting, "Push it up!"

And that's what we did, so the other team was gasping for air after just ten minutes. The game was as good as won. It was just a question of how big, and the score would already have been a lot bigger if Doc Naismith hadn't come up with a stupid rule that we had to have a tip-off after every basket. It kept us from playing faster, but when I'd complained about that to Grandpa Joe once, he'd teased me. "So now you want to reinvent the game, Calvin?"

Okay, so I didn't make the rules, but I thought a guy as smart as Topper could see that he ought to put me in.

I'd wanted to show off my uniform to our friends, but it didn't look like I'd get into the game. And even though Barney was out there, he didn't get to do much except guard the other team.

"Flash, start warming up," Jack said. "I want you to show them some razzle-dazzle. Don't worry about the playbook."

I couldn't figure who he meant, but then I realized his eyes weren't on the players by the basket but on the reporters at midcourt. They were starting to pack up to leave.

"But I'm just supposed to—" I began.

Jack twisted his mouth up into a grin. "I know what Topper wants. But that's not what we need. We've got to compete with dish night at the movies. Folks pay money to be entertained, not to see grown men toss a ball around."

I looked uncertainly at him, wondering what I'd gotten into.

"It's my team," Jack said. "You do it my way." He hustled over to stop the reporters.

After the basket, he called time and sent me in for Hollywood. Topper looked annoyed because he was supposed to be the coach, but he didn't want to make a scene in front of the reporters.

I trotted onto the boards, aware of the bright lights. From the stands, I could hear Jean and the others cheering. As I passed Topper, he said, "Just do your job and leave it to us to win, kid."

The other guy was tall, but he had as much bounce as a wet dishrag, so the Professor got the ball and passed it to me. Topper called out the play and held up his fingers in the signal.

The Gym-Dandies were already jogging back as I dribbled the ball up on the run. I could hear my friends shouting at the top of their lungs, but their voices sounded thin in that cavernous space.

"Push it up, Lazybones," Topper bawled at me, and he set the play for me and the others.

I was already past him, so I was going to tell him to push himself up, but I held my tongue. I went even faster and wound up catching up with the Gym-Dandies while they were still taking their positions. It would have been so easy to drive to the basket, but I stopped to wait for the rest of the team and then fed it to Topper—and I never saw the ball again on that play, as the others passed it around among themselves. The other team got frustrated and started to edge forward to try to intercept the ball. And then Alphonse ran along the baseline, and Topper threw a pass over the other team's waving hands right into Alphonse's paws. Alphonse went up and laid it in sweet.

The next thing I knew, Hollywood was trotting in. I thought it was for one of the others, but he shrugged apologetically. "You're out," he said.

"I ran the play like Topper wanted," I said, puzzled.

"I know, but Jack's pretty mad," Hollywood said.

As I trotted off, I saw Jack glaring at me from the sideline. He got right to the point. "I told you: razzle-dazzle."

"But that wasn't the play," I said.

Jack jerked a thumb at himself. "I don't care. When you get a shot, take it. Topper doesn't own the team. I do."

I wouldn't have minded taking Topper down a notch. "You'll back me up?" I asked.

"Topper can jump in the lake. He's gotten too big for his britches, so why don't you help me teach him a lesson?" Jack grinned, and he began waving his arms at the reporters to stay a little longer.

When I went back in for Barney, we rotated positions on the team: Alphonse and Hollywood would be the forwards and I was going to be a guard with Topper.

The Gym-Dandies got the ball, but that was fine by me. Some guys don't like defense, but not me. It was the only time when it was legal to pick a pocket, and I liked seeing the stiff's face when he found he was slapping empty air instead of the basketball—the bewilderment and then the anger. I liked doing it so much that I kept on until his shoulders sagged and he gave up trying.

When the pass came to my man, he started to dribble to the left. From the corner of my eye I saw one of his team-mates setting up a pick; but the pick was slow as molasses, so it was easy to get around him. And as I passed, I kicked the pick's foot so that he lost his balance slightly. He took a step to get it back—and nudged his friend with the ball.

It wasn't much more than a bump, but it was enough to throw off the dribbler. The ball just seemed to hang in midair, so it was easy to tap it away.

"Way to go, Flash," Barney shouted approvingly.

Topper started to call out a play, but I was already driving up the court. When I laid the ball in, flashbulbs began popping.

No one had ever wanted my photograph before this. And I liked it.

No longer feeling like Topper's puppet, I grinned innocently at him as I strolled back to the tip-off. "There was no one around, so I took the shot."

"No one likes a hot dog," Topper growled.

Says him. He was just jealous.

The next time we had the ball, I brought it up quickly. Topper and the others had already taken their places, and he clapped his hands together loudly to get my attention. "Here."

But Jack had gotten into position too in the corner with the reporters. He waved a hand at me. It was in my range, so I drove around the key.

"Hey," Topper called.

One of the forwards came toward me, lifting his arms so that he seemed like a human tree. But after all those practices, I'd gotten my legs back. I stopped and jumped so I could see the basket above his hands for a moment and I let the ball go.

More flashbulbs popped so that it was like lightning had hit the court.

When I landed, I didn't see what happened, but I heard the sweet swish.

Even though the rest of the team was glaring at me, Jack gave me a thumbs-up. I grinned back at him. I just hoped the photographers had brought plenty of film and flashbulbs.

PART TWO

The Spotlight

CHAPTER | VII

The next morning, I asked Ah Lee for his newspaper, and for maybe the first time in his life, he gave something away! He was even sort of polite, calling my old man *my father* instead of *the old rummy*. The team photo was on page three of the sports pages, and I left it on the bureau near a bottle, where my old man was sure to see it. "Don't drink yourself to death," I said, looking down at him.

"*Z-aw-p*," he snored.

When I heard the *a-rooga*, I took a last look around the storage room because that's what you're supposed to do when you leave your home, and then maybe you turn on the waterworks. But I didn't feel anything, so my eyes were dry. It was just a room full of boxes that stunk of an old wino, so I picked up my duffel bag and left.

And when you leave home in all those American and Chinese books and movies, your family's supposed to wail and carry on. But they've got to be awake and sober. Look at him—he was just sleeping off another bottle. Still, he was my old man, so I bent and kissed his cheek, holding my breath so I wouldn't smell the whiskey reek.

I never saw the hand that slapped me. "Get away from me," he snarled. He'd only been pretending to be asleep. He sat up, holding an empty bottle by the neck, ready to swing it.

I was going to hit him back, but wouldn't that have been something—climb into the car with a black eye or bleeding because he broke a bottle over my head? So I just retreated a couple of steps.

"I'm leaving," I said.

He blinked, bleary-eyed. "You still going ahead with this crazy scheme?"

"Yeah, ha-ha! You're going to have to balance the books yourself from now on," I warned him.

"You're going to wind up dead in the middle of nowhere." He waved his free hand vaguely toward the rest of the United States.

"Like father, like son," I said bitterly. "Without me, you'll die in the gutter."

"So?" he demanded surlily. "You're born alone; you die alone."

"You got that right," I said, and headed out the door for good.

Ah Lee nodded to me at the counter. "You show them, Calvin," he said.

I wasn't used to compliments. "Uh, thanks," I said.

Back in the storage room, I thought I heard the old man crying. Well, as slaps went, he'd hit me a lot harder.

I didn't owe him anything because it'd been Grandpa Joe and Uncle Quail who had been my real fathers. My old man had been an anchor around my neck all these years. Still, I was glad Grandpa Joe was going to make sure he was okay.

After all the hoopla and fancy talk from Jack, I had been expecting some grand touring car, or at least the one he'd been driving. It turned out, though, that he'd just borrowed the car that I had seen him in. All we had now was an old jalopy on which Jack had slapped a new coat of paint—which might have been the only thing holding its parts together. Four Boy Scouts would have felt squeezed inside it—let alone seven adults and their stuff.

Then Barney leaned over Hollywood and poked his head out the window. "I thought your ugly mug would have broke the photographer's camera."

I reminded myself this was an adventure. I managed to cram my duffel bag into the trunk somehow and then sardine myself into the backseat. Jack was at the steering wheel, so he twisted around to look at me. "You ready for the thrill of a lifetime?"

"It's in my blood," I said.

The exhaust fired like a pistol shot and the car chugged forward. The others didn't have much to say to me. I guess they were sore that my picture got into the paper; well, that was too bad. I'd only done what Jack had said.

Pretty soon, though, Alphonse began to sing "Tumbling Tumbleweeds" in a pleasant tenor voice and a bunch of other songs.

I felt like I was escaping from prison when we headed south away from Chinatown and San Francisco and past the orchards and sleepy fruit stands that lined either side of 101. We were beginning our tour in the hick towns, where we could play some local yokels in some school gym. Jack figured they'd be like scrimmages where we could fine-tune the team before we started to meet the good clubs.

It was slowgoing because even though 101 was called a highway, it was just a glorified name for a two-lane road. Every time someone made a left turn, it brought traffic to a standstill. When we got to the mountains, I thought we'd have to get out and push the car.

Hollywood started calling the jalopy Annie because she swayed from side to side just like the hips of the Chinese American actress, Anna May Wong. Pretty soon we were all begging Annie to make it up one more steep incline, and somehow she made it to the summit.

We hadn't seen a peep of the sun the whole day under the overcast November sky, and mist hung in tattered streamers from the tall redwoods that stood like silent green sentinels guarding the ocean. It was even darker as we wound our way onto the flat coastlands where I saw artichoke and strawberry plants in the rich soil like little green pom-poms sewn to black velvet.

"I know this road," I said. "Are we playing in Concepcion?"

"Give the gent a cigar," Topper said sarcastically.

"I've played pickup games there," I said. "They're not bad."

"You've never played with us before," Alphonse said airily. Barney and I just exchanged looks.

Concepcion was the heart of the coastal farmlands. Some days the air would be fragrant with the garlic and the onions growing in the fields. The main street to town was three blocks long and last time I had visited Uncle Quail, there'd been a lot of stores boarded up, the sidewalks filthy, and the folks looking worn out by all their cares. There were even more stores closed now, the sidewalks filthier, and the folks even more worn out. However, every street lamp and window had the team's posters.

Jack's mouth stretched into a wide grin, and he slowed the car as he hit the horn.

A-roo-ga, Annie honked out in a friendly fashion.

But for all the attention the sad-eyed people paid us, we could have been a truck filled with turnip crates.

A-roo-ga, a-rooga. Jack kept tapping the horn. "Wave," he told us.

"Why?" Alphonse joked. "You hot? You want us to fan you?"

"You're not six guys from Chinatown anymore," Jack explained. "You're celebrities who are here to make the miserable burghers of Concepcion forget their troubles for one evening. Tonight there's no mortgages, no overdue bills—just us and our show. So wave!"

Though we all felt foolish, we started to wave our hands. A smiling Jack kept slapping the horn. Heads turned to stare at the maniacs raising such a racket.

"I don't know if we're making the town happy," Alphonse said, "but we're certainly waking them up."

It was late afternoon, so we drove straight to the school; and while Jack went off to glad hand the newspaper editor, we went through a practice. But first Barney and me had to unload all the gear from the car.

The Professor's bag weighed a ton. "What've you got in here?" I puffed. "Rocks?"

"Knowing the Professor, he's got a change of socks and the rest are books," Hollywood said, stacking his on top of the load in my arms.

Topper saw how my legs were bowing under the weight, and he turned to the Professor. "I told you that you only could take two books."

"Two books would never last me for four months,"

the Professor protested and tried to share the shame. "Anyway, Hollywood is just as bad. I bet his bag's full of combs and Brylcreem."

"I've got to look good for the ladies," Hollywood sniffed, slicking back his shining hair. "And Alphonse probably has his stuffed with whoopee cushions and buzzer rings."

Alphonse looked wounded. "You forgot the fake vomit. It's a riot."

Somehow Barney and I staggered after the team into the gym where the Professor was taking a variety of shots at a basket. "The other one's okay, but the rim's soft on this one."

Topper rubbed his chin. "Okay, so the ball won't bounce so far on rebounds."

Then the Professor methodically began to walk around the court, testing the floorboards. "The wood's dead here," he said, pointing to a spot a few paces to his left. "Watch it when you dribble." He went around the rest of the court, telling the team what he had discovered as if he were as smart at reading a court as he was a book.

I took in the lecture sullenly. After carting in his bag of books and everything else, I felt like they were just using me the way that everybody else in Chinatown did.

"You listening?" Picking up a basketball, Topper whipped it at me.

I barely brought my hands up in time to catch it, but Topper's throw left my palms numb. "Yeah."

When we started practicing, Topper rode me extra hard. According to him, I couldn't do anything right.

He only let up when Jack got back with a paper bag. "Thanksgiving is on me today, but after this you buy your own meals." He took out enough turkey sandwiches for everyone.

Suddenly aware of how hungry I was, I tore the wax paper off my sandwich. "Thanksgiving's the last week in November."

"Don't you read the papers?" the Professor asked. "Roosevelt made it the third Thursday this year instead of the fourth so folks would have more time to shop for Christmas presents."

Alphonse laughed harshly. "With what?"

"That's right," Jack said. "All across the country, everybody's going to be spending their two bits to see you play." He kept a soft drink for himself and handed out the rest to the other Dragons.

"Where's ours?" Barney asked.

"You and Flash make tea," he said, leaning the bottle against a bench and popping the cap off with a jerk of his hand. "Paragraph—"

I groaned. "I know, I know, Paragraph ten, Clause five."

I had planned to throw the kettle away, but that would

have meant we were stuck drinking the rusty water coming out of the tap, so we wound up making tea anyway.

However, as we sipped our tea, the other Dragons chugged their sodas and then held a burping contest. Barney and I suffered in silence as we ate.

When everyone was done, I asked, "Is there going to be any more practice?"

Topper was already starting to nod his head when Hollywood gave a groan. "Have a heart, Topper. You're gonna run the legs off us before the game."

When the rest of the team chimed in, Topper gave up. "Okay. The rest of you take a break." He pulled a piece of chalk from his bag and jabbed it at Barney and me. "But you rookies diagram the plays. Show me what you learned."

"Aw, have a heart," I said. "I've got an old friend here. He's sort of like family." In fact, he'd been better family to me than my old man. There were times when my father'd disappear while he went on a bender, but Uncle Quail had left standing orders with Grandpa Joe to ship me down to Concepcion whenever that happened. "I'd like to give him a ticket."

"Quit being a wet hen," Jack said as he tore off a hunk of his turkey sandwich. "All work and no play makes Flash a dull boy."

"I'm the coach," Topper said.

As they stared at each other, Jack chewed his mouthful

as if he had all the time in the world. "And I'm the man-ager."

It was Topper who finally looked away, slapping his leg in disgust. "You better be back a half hour before the game."

Jack turned to me with a smirk. "Just give me his name and I'll make sure there's a ticket at the door for him. And I'll deduct the cost from your pay."

So I told him and then wrote down Uncle Quail's Chinese name too, but when I started to leave, Barney drained his tea and got up with his sandwich. He didn't want to be alone with Topper's bunch any more than I would have wanted to. "I'll go with you."

Eating our Thanksgiving dinner as we walked, we passed old wooden stores with faded signs that sold everything a farmer could want. The mountains we'd crossed cut off Concepcion from the big city stores, so a grocery shop might also stock overalls, books, and even sheet music for pianos.

"Wait," Barney said, and headed over to a small rack of postcards outside. "Gotta send in our salary to our agents. Grandpa Joe gave me some 'luck' money for the trip." He pulled out a small bright red envelope called a *li see*.

There were only three types of postcards, but Barney took his time selecting one as if it were a diamond. Too bad for him.

I took out the one that showed Main Street back before the Depression. All the stores were open and the sidewalks were clean. It didn't look like the present place at all. In fact, it could have been Anytown, U.S.A.

I checked the back and saw that it didn't say Concepcion, so I snagged the whole bunch. "Loan me some money, will you?"

"You only need one," Barney said, puzzled.

"Not the way I'm going to do it," I grinned. "Watch the master and learn, my son."

With the postcards bought and tucked into our pants, we headed on. The broken glass crunched under our shoes as we crossed into an area that was the wrong side of the tracks. The bars, though open, weren't busy just yet. In an open field, some hobos had set up a Hooverville—which was named in honor of the president who had presided over the start of the Depression. There were tents and makeshift shelters, but one fellow had the luxury of a piano crate.

It was funny to think that a kids' game meant I didn't have to live there.

Chinatown wasn't too much farther. The paint had worn off the boards of the stores and flophouses so that they were all a drab gray. When it was time to harvest crops, the place was hopping with Chinese farmworkers, but right now in November it was dead.

Still, there were some of them around—either they were too old or too poor to leave. Their faces had more wrinkles than the old asphalt of the street and some of them walked with a permanent stoop. A couple of them opened the door to a shed with a sign almost as big as it was that proclaimed it to be the Imperial Pleasure Palace. From inside the decrepit casino, I heard a dealer calling out for bets and the rattle of beans beneath the over-turned bowl. The players would have to guess if it was an odd or even number of beans under the bowl.

But these were the real old-timers, the true Guests of the Golden Mountain. They were probably the third generation to come over, but with the Japanese invading China, they couldn't go back even if they had the boat fare.

However, Jack had missed a bet. He hadn't bothered with the Chinatown. There wasn't one poster about us anywhere.

Barney sniffed the air. The cooks in the restaurants were already starting to fry up a storm for their customers. "Yeah, let's get some real food."

"You go if you want," I said. "I'm heading on."

Barney hid his disappointment and kept me company, but as we neared the ocean, it got colder and wetter—and smellier.

Barney wrinkled his nose in disgust. "Who's drying fish?"

"Uncle Quail," I laughed. "When I used to stay here, it would take months to get the stink out of my hair and clothes."

"How much can get on you in a few minutes?" Barney asked. He wasn't too happy about the notion.

Seen from above, the cove was pretty as a stained-glass window. The water was a blue so brilliant it almost hurt the eyes, and the cliffs around it formed a carved leaden frame. At the mouth of the cove was the reef where there were flashes of reds and pinks as the tide surged away to reveal the tide pools.

Beside a rickety shack were racks on the ledge with trays on which the small, flat flounderlike sand dabs were being dried and salted. And there were more down on the beach below. The air was thick with the pungent odor and Barney almost gagged, but it only took one whiff for me to get comfortable with it. I'd actually helped Uncle Quail salt the fish, and I'd slept in his house, which stank of the fish salting outside.

"Hey, Uncle," I called down to him.

Uncle Quail squinted upward and beamed when he saw me. "Cal-vin. You came after all. Where's your bag?"

"I'm just here for a quick visit," I called down. I headed down the rickety steps along the face of the cliff. Uncle Quail's shack was as close as I got to a home. "I brought a friend, Barney Young."

Uncle Quail leaned his head to the side while he thought a moment. It was a familiar tilt a Guest did when he was trying to see if he had any ties to you or your family. "Young, Young. I know a Joe Young."

"He's my grandfather," Barney said. If he'd had any hope of staying away from the stink, it was gone now. Once a Guest began figuring out his connections to you, it was like a spider spinning a web around you. I've known Guests to go back four generations and two continents as they figured out all the ways they were linked to you.

"His father came from *Three Willows* in China," Uncle Quail said, using the Chinese name. "I visited it once. It's a nice place. You should go there once we chase out the Japanese."

"Not me," Barney said. "I want toilets that flush."

By then, we had reached the ledge and I hugged Uncle Quail. Beneath his ragged clothes, his body felt like steel. There were piles of abalone shells on the porch, while his abalone iron hung by its wrist strap from a peg on the wall.

"I'll make you dinner in a moment," Uncle Quail said, "and then we can talk."

I was sorry to disappoint the old man. "We can't stay that long. We've got a game."

"Still playing basketball?" Uncle Quail said. "Why don't you come and work for me."

"Playing basketball is our job," I said proudly.

Uncle Quail gave a snort. "How?"

So we told Uncle Quail to his growing disbelief. "Who would pay to see a game?"

"Come and see," I said affectionately. "There'll be a ticket for you."

Uncle Quail stroked his scraggly goatee. "I will if I have the time."

Barney was turning blue from trying to hold his breath, but he let it out now in a whoosh. "The fish can wait."

"My visitor doesn't always come on time though," Uncle Quail said.

I spotted him first. It was a little brown dot on the surface surrounded by ripples. It passed through the gap in the reef across the mouth of the cove.

As Uncle Quail fed, he explained: "There used to be bunches and bunches of sea otters. Just like there used to be lots of Chinese. But then the Americans got rid of them like they did us."

"So that makes them our hairy cousins?" Barney joked. He ran a hand through his hair.

Uncle Quail held out a strip of abalone to Barney. "Your great-grandfather was also named Otter."

"I didn't know that," Barney said, scratching his cheek sheepishly.

Uncle Quail shook his head. "Young people are too impatient to hear about their own families. But that makes this fellow a sort of cousin."

"I guess," Barney said, taking the strip and flinging it over. "Here, cuz."

The strip turned end over end and splashed a yard away from the otter that dove and reappeared upon its back, the strip clutched in its paws.

Uncle Quail rummaged around on a rack for more abalone and fish. "The less you know about the past, the more alone you'll feel. You think you're the only one who's gone through this stuff—but you're wrong. The same problems pop up over and over through the generations." He nodded toward the reef. "You wait until low tide and I'll take you out to the reef so you can see the tide pools."

"I've never seen one," Barney said wistfully and looked at me.

I shook my head. "But I don't think we have time." And the water would be way too cold for Barney and me, who didn't have the seallike hide of Uncle Quail.

Uncle Quail looked disappointed. "Maybe next time I can show you." He shaped a circle with his hands. "All those animals are in their own separate worlds, but there're little streams of water that link them even if they don't see it. No one's alone." There were times when he and Grandpa Joe could sound a lot alike.

Uncle Quail gave Barney a shorter version of the same spiel he'd given me over the years about how all we Chinese were connected. He'd been good to me so I always put up with it, and Barney was used to being lectured by old-timers like Grandpa Joe, so he nodded his head periodically while not paying attention as he fed his "cousin."

The lecture was the price you paid for visiting his cove, but it wasn't like I believed any of it. I felt bonds to Uncle

Quail and Grandpa Joe, Barney, and our girlfriends and their families, and even, reluctantly, to my old man, but that was where it ended. The rest of the world didn't care about me, and I didn't care about it, so there was no good preaching to me about hugging strangers just because they were my fellow humans, and as for Guests, they had spat at me as gutter trash.

Long ago, I'd perfected the technique of paying attention to Uncle Quail, but I was actually drinking in the view one last time. This was the one place where I always felt at peace. The setting sun finally slipped beneath the clouds and suddenly the dreary, slate gray sea began to sparkle and deepen in color; and as the light spread across the waves into the cove, the water here turned to a turquoise more blue than any jewel I had seen. The brilliant sea made the beach sand gleam as white as sugar. I caught glimpses of color from the reef, and I was sorry the tide wasn't lower because it would be worth braving the swim through the cold water to see the creatures there. But maybe it was just as well. I'd be tempted to stay. And I had bigger fish to fry—if Jack was telling the truth.

"We'd better get back," I said.

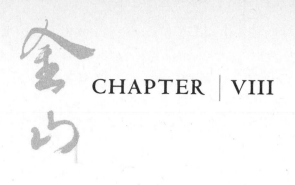

CHAPTER | VIII

It was no big deal to the others who were used to school locker rooms, but I hadn't been on a school team for very long, so it was exciting to pull on my uniform there even if the lockers were rusty and the air smelled of stale sweat.

The jersey went on fine, but I couldn't get my right leg through my shorts. That was funny because they had fit okay in the exhibition game at Kezar. I wound up hopping on my left leg like a mad stork.

"What's wrong, Flash?" Alphonse asked. "Your leg swell up too big for your pants?"

I sat down as the other Dragons began to laugh. "Ha-ha. Very funny." When I checked the shorts, I saw that the opening on the right side had been sewn up.

"I warned you he liked to play practical jokes," Hollywood said.

"Remember the time I put white shoe polish into the Brylcreem bottle?" Alphonse asked, relishing the memory.

"It aged him thirty years," Topper chuckled.

"And me with a hot date that night," Hollywood mourned. "She took one look at me and told me, 'I don't date grandpas.' And then she left."

"Here, Cal." Good old Barney had taken a razor blade from his bag, and I used it to cut the stitches as Barney went on to make tea. "If it's what got my family through the railroad and coal mines, it ought to get us through this trip."

Then Topper used matches and bottle caps to go over the plays one last time. From the street outside, I could hear car and truck motors in increasing numbers, and just beyond the wall the voices of fans as they gathered inside the gym—it started as a murmur that grew steadily into a growl from a giant throat.

Jack came to the door with a basketball in his hands. "It's time, guys." And he tossed it to Topper.

The ball seemed made for Topper's hand as he dribbled first through the door. We'd also practiced our entrance and we hit the gym on the run, dribbling and passing the basketball. The other team was warming up at the opposite end of the gym, but no one was watching them. We didn't do anything fancy, but people applauded anyway. I gazed up at the stands. No more sad, hopeless faces. They looked excited and determined to enjoy themselves.

Maybe Jack knows what he's talking about, I thought to myself. People really seemed to be forgetting their troubles.

"Up the Chinese!" Uncle Quail shouted in Chinese, and a cheer went up.

I twisted my head and saw him in the stands. Around him were a couple of dozen Guests. I guess he'd gotten the word out.

"Heads up!" Hollywood yelled.

The next moment the ball hit me hard in the chest and bounced off in a high arc that Topper caught as if we'd actually rehearsed that. It brought a big laugh.

"I guess we'll keep that routine," he grinned and dribbled over to our basket.

When the game started, I was on the bench with Jack. "Topper picks on you because he's the top dog, but not for long," he assured me.

"I can defend myself," I said, but I felt like there was a bruise just above my sternum.

"You going to fight him after school?" Jack asked sarcastically. "You do what I say, and you're going to be the leader of the team instead of him."

I wanted to ask him how he was going to make that happen, but by then the game had started and Jack set me to my other task. He had me sit on the end of the bench nearest to the timekeeper. "No rest for the wicked. The sixth man has to keep an eye on the timekeeper," he explained. "I once played the longest ten seconds of my life in a game because the keeper wanted to give enough time for the home team to beat us. I think ten minutes went by on my watch."

The other team called themselves the Concepcion Cavaliers, but I'd never heard of them before. Chances are they were a team that had been put together for the game, so they were a notch above the pickup teams I'd played against in the playgrounds here. They might know one another, but they probably hadn't played together as one team, which meant they wouldn't have many plays and wouldn't even run those well.

Some of them had the leathery faces and callused hands of field workers, but they all looked like they'd been picked for heft and height and could have been a pretty good offensive line for a football team. One of them was a Japanese kid I'd known from a pickup game up in San Francisco—Teddy Furumoto. I guess he'd moved down here, and the American diet must have agreed with him because he was five-eleven.

Still, though they were slow, they knew their basics. And when they spread their arms, they seemed as wide as they were tall, so it was hard to drive in on them as well as shoot over them. When the Dragons could get a rebound, they were fast enough to get ahead of the Cavaliers, but there weren't many of them. The Cavaliers waited until they had gotten a big man under the basket for an easy layup. The score was low and though we were ahead, it was only by a couple of baskets. Jack was chewing his lip nervously. Finally, he told me to go in. "Go get 'em, Flash."

I went in for Hollywood, who shot me a funny look. So did the rest of the Dragons. It was like they were waiting for something. I figured they'd be grateful for some of my razzle-dazzle.

The Cavaliers got the tip-off, but it was easy to steal it from the guard. The problem was the Cavaliers were so slow, they hadn't moved very far toward our basket, so it was easy for three of them to go on defense.

Behind me I heard Topper shouting out a play, but I thought of what the newspapers said and I thought of Uncle Quail and the other old-timers in the stands—especially the Guests who had scolded me for playing games. When I'd been on the bench, I'd heard Uncle Quail explaining basketball to them.

And I thought of the rest of the spectators too. They'd paid money to see this game. Jack had said it was about showing them a good time, so that made the court like a kind of stage. Do actors stumble out and just mumble their lines? Or do they put on a show?

So I didn't pull up like Topper wanted and pass the ball to him. Instead, I drove on ahead. It felt like running full speed through a forest of big trees, but then I was in the clear right beneath the basket. I banked the ball against the backboard so that it dropped through the net smooth as silk. As the ball bounced on the floorboards, I became aware of the roar from the stands. The spectators didn't care which team did the fireworks.

On the way back to the tip-off, though, I saw Topper talking to one of the Cavaliers, but I figured that he was just letting off a little steam. However, that Cavalier motioned for the others and spoke to them until the referee got mad and told them to play the game.

It was funny, but the Professor and Alphonse hardly tried to get the ball, so the Cavaliers got the tip-off easy. We fell back into position, so I thought they'd stop and begin passing it around in that patient offense of theirs, but their guard just kept pounding forward like he was a bull and I was a red cape. I set my feet and took one for the team, but the collision sent me sliding backward on my backside for a couple of yards.

"You can't do that," Uncle Quail yelled angrily in Chinese from the stands. He shouted a lot more. Grandpa Joe had once said Chinese poetry goes back for over four thousand years, but it can't hold a candle for creativity and imagination to Chinese curses, and inside Uncle Quail was a frustrated poet. He ended his tirade by advising me to "Chop off their heads!" He added a few details about what would happen to the head after that.

The next time we got the ball, I passed off to Topper, who was open—only to see him practically hand it to his opponent. The Cavaliers didn't try to fast break but moved it up slowly, so it was easy for the Dragons to get into our defense again. The funny thing was, it was a forward and not a guard with the ball—and he came at me like a battering ram.

I winced when I picked myself up off the floor. I now had matching bruises on both my chest and backside. "What did you say to them?" I asked Topper.

Topper tapped a finger against his chin. "I told them you were bad-mouthing them before the game. Let's see, I think the mildest insult I said that you said was that they had never seen toilet paper or indoor plumbing."

"You what!" I said.

"You wanted the attention, you got it, kid." Topper winked.

I took a real hammering after that, but I wound up single-handedly putting them in the team penalty. Still, we were actually down a couple of baskets.

Finally Jack called time, and when we'd gathered around him, he looked at Topper's sweaty face. "Okay, you made your point. Quit picking on the kid."

"You hiding behind Mama Jack now?" Topper asked me mockingly. And everybody but Jack and Barney laughed.

Jack was trying to take care of me like he had promised, but this wasn't really helping. I pretended to be humble. "I got the message. It's a team sport."

Topper grunted, "And I hate to lose." He glanced at his teammates.

They nodded their heads and Alphonse said, "I would have sworn a couple of times they had knocked you out. But you kept getting back up. You're a human cockroach."

"Or a jack-in-the-box." Topper grinned, but he conceded, "Take your shot when it's there."

I felt like I was one big bruise, but I was going to show everyone, including Topper, what I could really do. I forgot about my aches the first time I took my shot. When I peeked around the gorilla forward, I saw the ball bounce off the rim but then fall through the net.

We started to pull away after that. I may not have liked Topper any more than he liked me, but we'd have to work together if we were going to win, so if I had to give up a little of the spotlight, so be it.

I wouldn't say I was the smoothest cog in Topper's machine, but we worked well enough on defense. It didn't matter whether they tried to get the ball inside to their big men or took shots from the edges, we were just too quick for them. We managed to cut off passes or slap the ball away and disrupt the play.

They weren't good at improvising, and they began to get frustrated. They weren't in game shape either and began to tire. That all added up to mistakes that let us get our fast break going. Sometimes I took the shot, but I also passed it to the others and made sure they got their share.

By the fourth quarter the Cavaliers were so worn out from chasing us that they just crumbled. Or rather, they still had their will to win, but their bodies just couldn't meet the demands being made on them.

In the end, I felt a little sorry for the Cavaliers—but not that sorry. The score wound up being lopsided in our favor.

As we shook hands afterward, one of them even asked me for an autograph. "It's for my little girl," he shrugged. I saw her clinging to his jersey.

Jack was beaming as he talked with a reporter, but he called over to me. "Better get used to that."

I got Grandpa Joe's gift pen from my bag and signed my name with a flourish. As I was giving it to him, the crowd parted and I saw Uncle Quail walking toward me with a package in his hand. One whiff and I knew he'd brought me some of his salted sand dabs.

"Here," he said, thrusting it into my hands. "My friend wanted you to have some." I knew he meant the otter.

I liked his salted sand dabs a lot, but I didn't know how I could take them in our crowded car. On the other hand, I couldn't see how I could refuse them either. "Thanks. Did you enjoy the game?"

"You hopped around like a flea," Uncle Quail smiled. "You were like that even as a boy."

I laughed. "Is that why you were always making me swim in the cove when I wasn't working?"

"It was the only way to tire you out before you tired me out," Uncle Quail said, and patted me fondly on the shoulder. "You made me proud tonight."

Even though his fingers left a faint odor of salted sand dabs on my jersey, I didn't care.

"Flash, there's someone who wants to talk to you," Jack said. I turned to see he had the reporter in tow. I was going to tell Uncle Quail to wait a moment, but he had disappeared into the crowd like a shy shadow.

I'd no sooner greeted the reporter than Topper horned in. "We're still fine-tuning the team, but it's a good start." In shaking the reporter's hand, Topper boxed me out as neatly as he would an opponent under the basket. Cooperation only worked during a game; he wasn't about to surrender the spotlight to me.

Jack kept trying to steer the reporter back to me, but Topper always found a way of interrupting or taking over the answer. Suddenly I had an idea, so I slipped away and went to the locker room. The others were showering, so I wrote *From a fan* on the paper bag and then slipped the salted sand dabs into Topper's bag.

He deserved the rewards that came with the spotlight as well.

CHAPTER | IX

We had to drive all night to get to our next game. By midnight, the pungent smell of salted sand dabs had filled the car so bad that Jack, who had been trying to nap while Topper spelled him at the wheel, insisted we pull over. We were all still feeling the glow of our first victory, so there were a lot of grinning faces as we went through our luggage.

As Topper held the fish up, Jack pinched his nose and backed away. "I bet it's one of the soreheads on that other team. I once played with a Swede who ate salted fish just like that."

"I'm looking closer to home." Topper eyed Alphonse.

"I swear it wasn't me," Alphonse protested.

Barney scratched his head. "I dunno. It kind of makes me want a bowl of rice."

He shut up when I elbowed him. "Everything reminds you of food," I growled.

"I ate enough salted fish as a kid," Topper said as he flung the fish away. "Never again." He tried to wipe off his fingers on some grass on the roadside. "Man, I bet I got fish oil all over my clothes too."

Hollywood jerked a thumb at Barney. "Give him a bowl of rice, and he'll eat them."

Jack was already getting in the car. "Let's go."

"We ought to air out the car first," Alphonse said. We'd left all the doors open when we had exited the car.

Jack waved a hand impatiently. "We'll roll all the windows down. We gotta get to the next town."

Everybody was still feeling good from our first victory, so they didn't complain but piled back into the car. Hollywood was the last as he checked his hair and mustache in Annie's side mirror.

But man, was it cold with the wind blowing through the open windows; so I was sort of glad we were all packed together because the body heat kept me warm. Still, I don't know how sardines manage to sleep. I'd just start to drift off when somebody's head or elbow or even foot would jar me. And the snoring! I thought I was in a lumber mill with all the huge buzz saws spinning.

By dawn, we'd chugged our way into a little cow town. From the stink in the air, the four-legged animals must have outnumbered the two-legged ones, so maybe it was cattle or dairy cows. We had enough time to wash up in a gas station restroom sink and grab a quick bite at a roadside diner before we went to the gym.

After we practiced, Barney sat in the locker room to write his postcard to Tiger, thinking carefully about every word. On the other hand, I began to dash off the cards, using the fancy pen from Grandpa Joe.

On the first, I scribbled, *Things are okay, if you like cows and trees.* On the next, I wrote, *Ha-ha, what do you know? They were selling the same postcard. Who wants to make a separate card for every hick town? When you've seen one Main Street, you've seen them all.*

I kept writing similar things on all the other postcards until Barney looked over at me. "What're you doing? Writing *War and Peace*?"

"I'm doing them all right now," I said, writing away.

Barney frowned. "You owe Jean more than that."

"She's a buddy. She'll understand how busy I am," I said, continuing to scribble.

"She's more than that," Barney said quietly.

My pen jerked across a card, spoiling it. "I don't need anyone that much."

"Everyone needs somebody," Barney insisted.

Annoyed, I tore up the card. "Not me. I made up my mind when I was a kid."

Barney was getting to be a real pest. "Don't judge everyone by your father. Jean'd never hurt you."

I threw the pieces at him. "Mind your own business, will you?" I tried to change the subject. "Maybe we should stick to Paragraph ten, Clause five, after all," I said to Barney. "We have to make tea anyway, and it's free."

"It'll make our allowance go further," he agreed.

The game was in a dance hall where chicken mesh had been put up to protect the customers. Jack said other places had done that when he was still playing. It was like being in a cage, and that's how basketball players had gotten the nickname of cagers.

When the game began, I was on the bench with Jack again. We were up against the Pipers. They'd gotten their name not because they were a bagpiper band but because they were sponsored by a plumber, and they all plodded as if their feet were made of lead. "Make sure that the others get the ball as much as Topper," he instructed me.

"That's not how most of the plays work," I said. "Topper's the shooter."

"Topper can't object if you're keeping the others happy," Jack said. "They won't be trying to teach you a lesson like the last time."

By the time I went in, though, the burger sat heavy in my stomach, so it felt like I was trying to run with a thirty-pound melon in my gut. Topper had slipped around his man and was already heading toward the basket. He raised his hands expectantly as he looked over his shoulder at me.

I stared straight at him as I dished the ball to my left to Alphonse, who was in the clear beneath the basket. It was hard to say who was more surprised that he had gotten the ball—him or Topper, but he pivoted and made the basket.

Topper looked like he'd just swallowed a sour lemon, but he couldn't say anything. And he didn't say anything when I kept passing to the others. But outside of Barney, I was still learning where my teammates were going to be on a play because it worked a lot different in a game than in practice. My passes missed their targets more than I liked, but we still won a laugher.

Topper had the savvy to have brought along some photographs of himself and even managed to sell a couple of them with his autograph afterward—except the ones with fish oil on them. While he did that, the other Dragons patted me on the back.

Topper didn't say anything to me afterward when we got into the car, but all of us tried to sleep because it was an all-night drive. By the time I woke up, we were leaving a mountain range and I saw the sea stretching like blue glass away from a huge town. But as we passed through it, I saw it was mostly shacks that were shuttered up. I guess in the summer it hopped with tourists, but this was the off-season. Most of it was a ghost town except near the coast. The full-time inhabitants lived there in old houses eaten away by the salt air. Everywhere I looked I saw nets hung up to dry, either from poles or trees or being repaired, and the bay was filled with fishing boats.

"Bet there's more salty souvenirs for you, Tops," Hollywood called from the backseat.

Topper hadn't had a chance to wash his clothes yet and was wearing a shirt with an oily spot on it. He glowered at Hollywood so fiercely that Hollywood shut up. Then he muttered to Jack, "There better be a burger joint somewhere."

This time we played a team of local all-stars named after the sponsor, the Alioto Wholesalers, in a part of a warehouse near the dock. Though it had been cleared, the floor still stunk of fish—which might have put off some of their opponents but not players who still had the smell of *bom yee* in their nostrils.

A couple of guys looked like they'd barely cracked twenty-one, but there was one who could have been a classmate of Tiger's grandmom. They couldn't hit a barn with the basketball, but could they rebound! They went for the ball like it was a tuna flapping on a boat deck. They were all thin, so even if they were taller than us, I bet they didn't weigh any more, and it felt like they had sharpened their knees and elbows.

We ought to have beat them easy too, but the warehouse floor was "dead," so that balls barely bounced off it. The hoops had been hung from the rafters on real backboards about a foot lower than regulation height, but the Professor had "read" the place so we were prepared.

On the other hand, the lines for the court had been chalked on the floor by the referee, and the Wholesalers had this nifty little trick of erasing them with a swipe of their shoes so he couldn't tell what was out-of-bounds or where the key was. The last trick made it hard to tell when one of their players was loitering beneath the basket for more than three seconds, making it easier for them to get a good shot.

The poor ref just about ran out of breath from having to blow his whistle so often for an official time-out while he redrew the lines—until Alphonse managed to pick his pocket and steal his chalk. Then it was anyone's guess when a ball was out-of-bounds.

We still won, but they had crashed into us so much, we used up all the liniment on our bruises.

Aching from head to toe, we headed south into farm country, where there were more Martian-looking artichokes. The Professor and some of the others had also played football for some Chinatown outfit and had come down here once to play another club.

Our opponent that night was a team called the Bakers, and they had a guard who was speedy as a cockroach, so I got in early to take a turn at trying to stop him. When they set a pick for him, I felt like I was running into a stone pillar. The whole team was that way—like they'd been carved out of stone. And they didn't feel any softer when I tried to slice to the basket and one of them stomped in front of me.

To add insult to injury, the referee was a local guy who wouldn't call fouls on his friends, but he delighted in calling a foul on us every chance he got. The whole first quarter, all he did was call fouls on us, blowing his whistle shrilly and flailing his arms.

Jack, though, had an answer for that from his playing days, and he told me what to do. "Only make it seem like it's your idea, kid."

So when I went in, I motioned the others over for a quick huddle. "Let's do to the ref what you did to me in the first game."

"He'll call fouls," Topper objected.

"Not for long," I said. "Either he gets the point, or he'll be heading for the hospital."

Hollywood grinned. "I like it." And when the others nodded, Topper went along reluctantly.

After the next jump ball, the Professor seemed to stumble and crashed like a falling redwood right on top of the referee, who was a little guy. Then the Professor took his time getting up and maybe even dug in an elbow or two.

So the ref thought he'd get even, and as soon as he could during a play he called a foul on Topper. He got Lesson Two after the next jump ball when Topper and

Hollywood went for the ball from opposite sides. It didn't matter that the ball was bouncing ten feet away. Their real target was the ref, and when they crashed into him I thought he'd be as flat as the baloney in a sandwich.

He was so woozy after that, that for a while he'd be looking at one end of the court when we were playing in the other. But even if he still didn't call fouls on his team, he stopped calling them on us, so there was so much blocking and tackling that it was more football than basketball.

By the second half, we were all moving a little slower from all the collisions. We won the game but not by much, and we stumbled out of there, feeling like human pinballs.

Jack wasn't happy. He chomped at the stub of an unlit cigar so that it twitched up and down like a little tail. "You gotta play better than that if we're going to draw crowds. You gotta give them a show."

Topper was searching through the trunk for a bottle of liniment he might have missed. "We filled two-thirds of the bleachers." He straightened in disgust and jerked a thumb down a street. "I think I saw a drugstore back there. You got to get us some liniment."

"We can't throw money around yet. The house wasn't big enough. I wound up papering half the seats even though the publicity cost an arm and a leg." Jack slammed the trunk down. "The whole car still reeks like a hospital. Just wave your arms around."

"That's not the part that hurts." Barney tried to rub his backside and winced.

"Put up with it," Jack said sourly as he headed toward the driver's seat, "until we start filling all the seats."

"The contract calls for adequate medical care," Topper argued.

"You want medical care?" Jack asked sarcastically. He blew a kiss toward Topper. "Here. Put this on your boo-boo and make it feel all better."

That only set off Topper. The argument got louder until Barney finally offered, "I've got some Lion Salve that my grandpa gave me."

I groaned because as modern as Grandpa Joe was, that traditional remedy was his one blind spot. However, Topper insisted on stopping the car, and Jack finally did it just to shut him up. Then Barney, who was in the middle, crawled across everyone and out through the window that Hollywood, who was sitting next to it, rolled down for him.

"Put the window back up," Jack said with a shiver. "It's cold."

"Keep it down," I warned. "You'll be glad of the fresh air in a moment."

Barney got the small jar from his bag in the trunk and scrambled back into the car. Unscrewing the lid, Topper dipped his fingers into the jar, smearing it over various body parts—not an easy thing to do in a crowded car while it was moving. Then he passed the jar around until that itty-bitty jar got scraped dry by the team.

In no time, the fumes filled the car worse than the salted fish had. Jack took one of his hands from the wheel to cover his nose. "What died?"

"Our contract," Topper groused. "Right, guys?"

As the team nodded their heads grumpily, I realized what Topper's real game was. It wasn't about the liniment. He just wanted an issue that would drive the wedge between the team and Jack.

I guess Topper also knew how to play more games than basketball.

We headed back over the mountain range after that but this time into orchard country. In the moonlight, the bare trees looked like broken bones, miles and miles of them.

It was Barney's turn to sit next to the window. "Who'd a-thunk there was so much to California."

This time the gym was jammed to the rafters, and Jack craned his neck to scan the crowd. At the time, I figured he was taking a head count to check against our cut because we got part of the house. I would have said that maybe a quarter of the audience were Mexicans, but there were at least a dozen Chinese with faces burned into a mahogany color by the sun. Topper surveyed the crowd approvingly. "Barney, make sure you get some photos out of my suitcase."

The other Dragons knew the team, the Windmills, because they had played them in some tournament before. In the huddle before the tip-off, Topper said, "We've got to be at our best, guys. The Old Fox is here." He turned to Barney and me. "He's been teaching at the high school here since Noah's flood, so everybody here has trained in the same system."

Alphonse looked at the other bench. "Looks like he's come out of retirement to coach the Windmills tonight."

I think they have a special mold for some coaches. He was a tall man with a potbelly in a sweatshirt and a whistle with a strap that had probably fused into his skin. Whenever they cast a coach, they always left out the smile muscles.

Topper sighed. "He probably didn't like the way we trounced his boys last time."

It didn't matter whether they were eighteen or forty, each Windmill played like a cog in a machine. And the Old Fox had them playing the worst kind of style for us: They slowed everything down and set up in a box on the outside of the key and just passed the ball around like they were playing keep-away and not basketball.

They never shot at the basket, and the only way they scored was when we got sloppy and fouled them. And when we had the ball, they went into a zone defense and never let us have more than one shot. The moment one of us put up the ball, Windmills converged toward the basket to get the rebound, boxing us out.

Their style kept us from making baskets fast and kept the score low so they could keep up with us. After the end of the quarter, it was just ten to eight in our favor. It would be amazing if the final score broke thirty.

The disciplined style was slow and boring, but the crowd loved it because it was their boys pulling it off. Teenagers or grandparents, they clapped and yelled the same chants that they had all learned when they had attended the school. They stomped their feet on the bleachers until the gym shook like the inside of a drum. It had a real feel of a high school game and for the first time I really felt like it was us against the whole world.

It got even louder when they tied . . . and nearly broke my eardrums when they went up by a point on a foul shot. When Jack called time, the noise was still deafening.

By then, we were all feeling pretty tired and frustrated. Even Topper seemed glad of a breather.

Though Jack was standing right in front of us, he had to shout to make himself heard. "We're in trouble," he said.

"It stinks," Hollywood said, "but we were bound to lose a game."

"Not with them in the stands," Jack said and jerked his head at a half-dozen guys, some with boxy newspaper cameras. "I practically had to beg those reporters into coming. They're from towns we'll be playing in the near future. Flash has got to put on a good show tonight."

Topper frowned. "The All Stars are my team."

Jack's face got as hard and rough as asphalt. "You *were* the All Stars when you were amateurs, but I pay you, Tops, and everyone else. That means you're Dragons now. And if we don't win, we'll be lucky to earn enough money next week just for gas."

Topper glanced at the press and then relented. "Well, maybe just for this game."

Jack folded his arms. "The key is that young guard. He's the only real ball handler. Get him upset, and we break down that stall. Shake his cage first, Flash. I'll tell you when to go in for the kill."

"You might as well hang a target on Flash's back," Alphonse objected.

Jack watched me real close as if he had just handed me my final exam and, depending on what I said, it would be pass or fail. "Are you my boy, or aren't you?"

Well, as far as Chinatown was concerned, I was already trash. I shrugged. "What have I got to lose?"

When the game resumed, I immediately went to work on the young guard. He was right-handed like me, so I made him move to his left, which threw off his dribbling, passing, and shooting. And he liked to shoot in a certain rhythm, so I did everything I could to throw that off.

And whenever he made a bad play or I made a good one, I made sure to rub it in with smirks and whispers that only he and I could hear. That alone wouldn't have bothered him because there's always some banter that goes on in a game, and sometimes tempers get the better of judgment so their ball handler had probably heard plenty of insults before this.

But he'd never heard any stuff like what had been thrown at me. It was pure slime from the gutter with that poetical Chinese touch, and I'd heard plenty from Guests or landlords when they were evicting us.

I was careful, though, because of the reporters in the stands. Besides Jack, the only one who noticed what I was doing was the Old Fox, who'd been watching me the whole time. He wagged an index finger at me.

As if that could stop me. I was going to get that spotlight by hook or by crook.

The young guard started to get distracted; so he got called for traveling. Finally, he threw a pass too hard. When the ball ricocheted off his man's hands, I got it on a high bounce and had an easy run down to the bank where I could lay it up nice and sweet. And then on our way to the tip-off, I leaned in close and out of the side of my mouth, I thanked him softly for his mistake.

After that, he started getting more and more rattled, which made him sloppy and gave me a chance to steal the ball.

"Now, kid!" Jack shouted at me, and I saw him stomp his foot and then grind something under his heel. It was time to go in for the kill.

I raced down the court to the other basket, but instead

of making an easy layup, I stopped fifteen feet away and went up like a rocket to make my shot. And I heard a scattering of applause from the stands.

As I went back for the tip-off, I made sure to mouth another "thank you" to the Windmill guard. He just glared at me.

And when they got the ball, he didn't set up for his slow-down passing game and instead tried to drive past me for a basket of his own. But Alphonse and the Professor both closed on him and swatted the ball out of his hands.

Whirling around, I started the other way. From the corner of my eye, I saw Topper keeping pace with me on my left.

When a Windmill set up in front of me, I bounce-passed the ball through his legs to the Professor for an easy layup.

His coach wound up pulling him out of the game and lecturing him as he sat on the pine, but the guard just kept stewing anyway about what I'd done to him.

Jack had nailed it on the head: They weren't the same team without that young guard's skills. We got more balls and wound up going up by six. Mercifully, that quieted the crowd down too.

"Now, kid!"

And it was easy to put on a show with flashy passing and shooting and playground moves. Sure enough, the camera's flashbulbs started popping whenever I touched the ball.

The rest of the Windmills went after me, trying to foul me every chance they got. Once, I was driving toward the basket when a forearm came out like a signpost and caught me right in the throat.

I bounced back up like I was made of rubber, made the foul shot. If they thought they could intimidate me, they had another think coming. I'd taken a lot more punishment pulling my playground con.

The result was that the whole team got so mad at me, they forgot all about their system—and without it they were nothing but stiffs. And their foxy old coach was helpless to stop things from falling apart. On the bench, Jack was grinning like the cat that had eaten the canary, so I guess it was all part of his strategy.

The Old Fox wound up having to put back in his ball handler who hadn't calmed down any—and it was easy to stoke the boiler so he was really steaming. He said things to me in a loud voice, but I'd learned from my mistake long ago. I wasn't about to lose my big break, so I kept tight control of my temper and just continued to play so he'd look like the bad guy.

Finally, he tried to show me he could be as flashy as me, and swiping the ball from him was like stealing candy from a baby. On the way back to the tip-off, I let him know how grateful I was for his gift. It wasn't anything

I hadn't said to him before, but it was enough to set off his fuse.

Furious now, he flung himself at me with his hands stretched toward my throat. I could have dodged him easy, but that wasn't the point, was it? I leaned back enough so that my neck was out of his reach and we toppled over with him on top.

The upshot was that he got thrown out of the game at the cost of a couple more bruises on my chest. As I shot the technical that had been called on him, the crowd started to boo, but I saw Jack give me a quiet thumbs-up.

We wound up winning by seven, but I'd been knocked around so much that I knew how a flank steak must feel after the butcher's hammer had tenderized it.

The Old Fox made a beeline toward me. "Your team gave us a hard time, coach," I said, holding out my hand.

He just glared at it. "I'd like to say the better team won tonight, but I can't. You ought to be ashamed of yourself."

He made me remember all the reasons that I'd given up on school teams. "Maybe the game's passed you by, old man," I smirked. I hated myself even as I said it.

He sucked in his breath like I'd just punched him in the gut, but then he squared his shoulders. "Not if I can help it. The game's about character, not about winning."

"It's about filling seats," I said and walked away toward the rest of my team.

Alphonse trotted up. "Jack says he'll have the motor running."

"But we got to shower," Hollywood protested.

Topper waved to some of the Chinese who were making their way slowly down the bleachers toward us. "And I got photos to sell."

"Forget your photos, Tops," the Professor said, and jerked his head toward the small crowd gathering around the other team. "There's a lot of folks here who don't like us—and Flash in particular. If we don't leave now, we could be tarred, feathered, and ridden out on rails."

The Professor and Jack had already transferred our gear into the trunk of the car, and with the ugly looks we were getting, we all started to jog toward the door.

Only, Jack didn't have the car running like he'd promised. He ambushed us at the door with the reporters who wanted to interview us. Topper set up like he usually did, but they peppered me with questions instead. Topper got this sour look on his mug.

At first, I didn't quite know what to make of all the attention. I just wanted to get away, but after a while, it started feeling sort of nice. If you asked most folks in Chinatown, they would have predicted I was one step away from joining my dad in the gutter. I fed them the standard stuff that Topper usually did, but it was me doing the parrot routine and not him.

From the corner of my eye, I saw Jack form the letter

A with his fingers, so I figured I'd passed my exam. And he'd prepped the reporters so that they wanted to talk to his star pupil rather than Topper. True to his word, he was grabbing the spotlight for me, and it made it all the sweeter because he was snatching it from Topper.

By the time they let us go, there was a mob around the car. The other team hadn't bothered to shower either. They'd been too busy finding two-by-fours and lead pipes.

The group's ringleader was the spitting image of the ball handler—except older, so I assumed he was the ball handler's dad. "You think you're real sneaky, don't you, boy?" he asked as he slapped a tire iron against a calloused palm.

He then proceeded to prove he had a mouth just as foul as mine, and the ball handler, who was also there, began to spew all the things he'd been thinking but hadn't been able to say during the game: not just insults against me but against all Chinese in general and anybody with dark skin.

"We just want to leave, gentlemen," Jack said. He never saw the board that swung at him, but he reacted instinctively, so it took him in the shoulder instead of the head.

And then the mob surged toward us. It made me remember Grandpa Joe's stories about when he'd been stuck in Rock Springs and a mob had rioted there. And I began to think we'd be lucky not to get lynched.

A whistle suddenly cut through the air, cold and sharp like a knife, and a voice bellowed like a fog-horn. "Enough!"

I thought it might be a ref, but it was the Old Fox. As he stepped forward, he scolded, "I taught you boys better than that." Wherever he looked, heads hung in shame. "Now step back so our guests can leave."

Silently the mob opened a lane for us to the car. I saw they'd already taken out some of their anger on it because it had dents and a broken window.

Jack picked up his hat from the ground and led us toward the automobile. As I passed the Old Fox, I murmured, "Thanks."

He caught my shoulder and whispered to me, "Remember, boy: The Game is everything. You, me, none of us count." He made a point of escorting me past his former students, and though there were plenty of hostile looks shot at me, nobody tried anything. At the car, he let me go. "You don't have to be a thug. You've got a talent, boy. If you polished it, you could shine like gold."

Out of a show of defiance, I shot back some rude words at him, but as I squeezed into our dented car, I found myself wishing I could have had him as my coach. Maybe I could have been someone that I liked and respected too—and not some mug with nothing to lose.

Instead, what I had was Jack, but the Old Fox wouldn't like the kind of polish he was giving me. I'm not sure I did either.

CHAPTER | X

The Dragons headed northeast, rolling back through the mountain range and then over another, so we had to sleep in the car even though sometimes we were sliding back and forth on the curves. Because we hadn't had a chance to shower before we left, the car began to stink almost as bad as it did with the salted fish and the Lion Salve. But I felt like most of the stink came from me. The Old Fox's words gnawed away at my insides like bugs.

So between him and the squirming and elbowing of the rest of the sleeping team, I didn't catch many z's. By dawn, I just gave up.

"Where are we?" I mumbled to Jack, who was at the wheel.

"Just heading out of the last mountain pass," he blinked sleepily. "That's the San Joaquin Valley ahead."

I twisted so I could see over the seat. Once it cleared the slope, the highway shot straight as an arrow past the green and brown patches that were fields. The mist had smudged out the horizon, so the road didn't seem to have an end. As the sun rose, it seemed to glow and pulse.

"It just doesn't seem to end," I said.

"That's because it's the Dragon Road," Jack said. "Our road."

"Never figured you to be a poet," I yawned.

"Guess I'm just a little batty from all this driving." He looked embarrassed and tried to change the subject. "You didn't sleep too well. Something bothering you, kid?"

"Nothing," I insisted.

"I saw that old coach talking to you," Jack said shrewdly. "Did he say something to upset you? Consider the source: He's slaved away all his life for small change, so his idea of a big treat is the blue plate special at the local greasy spoon. And you know why? So he can be the big frog in the small pond. He's just jealous."

"Yeah?" I asked.

Jack nodded. "I've met jerks like that everywhere I played. The only way they can feel good is by making you feel bad."

I sat up, reassured. "Yeah." And I believed him because I wanted to.

"Old Jack is the only one you have to listen to," he told me. "Have you been sending your agent her commission?"

"Yeah, I've been mailing postcards," I said.

"Good," he grunted. "I'd rather tangle with a pit bull than her again."

As we drove through the valley, we found ourselves in the middle of wheat farms that could have been ripped out of Kansas. Old frame farmhouses and barns and silos and fields, lying fallow after the harvest, stretching on forever like a brown sea.

We didn't stop until we reached the town where we were supposed to play a game that evening—though all of us were bone weary. In the diner, Bing Crosby was crooning that he had the world on a string. Well, so was mine, but it was a yo-yo string and right now it was stretched to its lowest point.

As we slid into the booth, Barney groaned, "My tail's so numb that I can't tell if I'm sitting."

"You're sitting," I grunted helpfully.

Jack bustled through the door with an armload of newspapers, which he passed out to us. "We made the front page, boys."

Hollywood was the first to snatch up a paper and look at it eagerly, but then he lowered it. "You mean Calvin made it."

Jack squeezed into the booth, forcing us to slide even closer together. "Can I help it if he's photogenic?"

"You'd think he'd won the game all by himself," Hollywood said sourly. He flung his copy down.

I opened the paper. Sure enough, they'd gotten me in mid-jump with the ball soaring out of my hand and angry, openmouthed opponents glaring up at me. The first line of the article said it all: "Last night a gang of Chinese bandits stole the ball, the show, and the world's attention, and the ringleader was a kid phenom, Flash Chin, who not only has larceny in his heart but more bounce than a jackrabbit. The crowd got treated to Hank Luisetti's new invention, the running one-handed shot. It won't be long before every player's trying to hop around like him."

So Jack had kept his word after all. I'd send the article on to Jean and Grandpa Joe. Maybe another copy to my old man. There was an outside chance he'd sober up enough to open my letter. I was proving him and all those Chinatown Guests wrong about me and basketball. I was finally someone important. Suddenly I began to hope for the first time in a long time.

However, I could see the rest of the team had their noses out of joint, so I made a point of shrugging it off. "It'll be your turn next time." I didn't really believe it, but if I was going to survive to the end of the tour, I'd have to get along with them.

"That's right," Jack said. "You boys listen to me and we'll all be in the chips. Anyway, what's good for one Dragon is good for all." He opened a menu to help hide his face before he winked at me. "Nothing like a front page to help the appetite."

154

"Depends on what you read," the Professor mumbled. The pages rattled as he turned them. "The whole world is going to war. Eventually the fighting between China and Japan has got to draw in the other Asian countries and colonies—and that means the British and us. And if they don't do it, then the fighting between England, France, and Germany will."

Hollywood nudged the Professor's elbow. "You're the only one who'd read the news before sports."

Alphonse poked a hole through a newspaper headline. "Aw, England and France don't really want to fight Germany, or they would have done it when the Nazis invaded Czechoslovakia last year."

"They declared war after Germany blitzkrieged Poland," the Professor argued. *Blitzkrieg* was the German word for the tank warfare that had ripped up the Poles two months ago.

Hollywood jumped in. "The British and French might have declared war, but they'll just twiddle their thumbs for a while and then everyone will claim they won and go home."

"Besides, even if the rest of the world goes crazy, America will mind its own business," Jack insisted, and it was a sentiment we all echoed. We laughed at the Professor for being a Gloomy Gus and left him to ponder the world's fate while we used the salt and pepper shakers from the tables around us to go over last night's game.

Even Professor Killjoy put down his newspaper to stoke up on an old-style farm breakfast with plenty of eggs, bacon, sausage, home fries, toast, and enough coffee to power a battleship.

For dessert, Jack handed out our pay. The others got twenty-five bucks, but Barney and I got only five each. "Hey, what gives?" I asked.

"Take it up with your agents. I send the rest to them." Jack grinned. "I think it's Clause five. You trust them to put it in the bank?"

"Does he trust you to send it?" Topper's voice came out muffled as he spoke into his coffee cup.

I was feeling too stuffed and sleepy to practice, but Jack said it would be good for us as we got into the car.

Everyone froze, though, when we heard the police siren. In San Francisco, the cops used to check Barney and me out just because we were Chinese outside of Chinatown and that was suspicious in itself. From the way the others stiffened, I think they had also been hassled at some time by the flatfoots as well. However, the police car sped past us until it caught up with a beat-up old jalopy piled high with battered suitcases and furniture that would have been better used as kindling.

A big bull of a cop got out and went over to the driver's side. They were finishing up their conversation as we slowly passed by in our car. "We don't want Okies here," the cop was saying.

The last few years, the farms in the Midwest had been so overfarmed the dirt had been worn out and began to blow around like dust. Oklahoma had been hard hit, but other states had gone through times just as bad. The banks had foreclosed on the farms, so that the farmers had to take to the road to find jobs. A lot of them had come from Oklahoma so they were called Okies, but they really came from all over.

The faces of the driver and the woman next to him had as many wrinkles as sun-dried mud. They looked as tired and worn-out as eighty-year-olds, but their blond hair suggested they were a lot younger than that. There were four kids piled into the back who looked just as tired and dirty.

"Nossum," the driver said. "We're just a-heading on." He paused hopefully. "Unless you know someone's hiring?"

The cop waved his thick nightstick. "Not here and not for the likes of you. Move on."

"Right, right," the driver said. He tried to start the engine, but it kept coughing. As we left them behind, he had jumped out and was desperately turning a crank on the front of the car to start it.

"There but for basketball go us," the Professor said gratefully.

I think everyone was glad we had the team when we got to the gym, but this time when Jack put up the trunk he motioned me back. "Barney can bring in the gear. Don't want to risk injuring Flash. Right, Barney?"

Barney hesitated but nodded. "Yeah, sure."

I knew the rest of the team was watching, though. I had enough bruises already without being taught another "lesson" about team play. "I'm feeling fine."

I started toward the trunk, but Jack caught my arm. "I said to let Barney do it."

"Go on in, Cal," Barney said. "I don't mind."

"Mr. Coughlan?" a middle-aged man asked. He was wearing a worn suit with a string tie.

"Game's not for a while," Jack said.

"I'm here on behalf of my friend, Mr. Young," the man said, and extended a hand. "I'm the Reverend Whittle. He wrote me to remind you to send his charges' salaries."

Jack looked taken aback for a moment and then muttered, "Now I know why they asked for the schedule."

The Reverend Whittle looked embarrassed. "I'm . . . ah . . . to see that you mail it."

"Don't worry, Reverend. I'll do it," Jack assured him with a slick smile.

However, the minister pointed to a church across the street. "But I've been asked to make sure you do. He even sent an envelope and stamp."

"Happy to oblige a man of the cloth." Jack sighed.

While Jack took care of business, the Professor did his usual routine of checking out the court and explaining its peculiarities to us and then we had a practice. And then Topper rode me hard, telling me over and over that I shouldn't believe my own headlines while the others all grinned.

By now, I was getting to know the Dragons' quirks as we sat in the locker room waiting for the game to begin. Barney, of course, was writing to Tiger; the Professor was lost in a history book thicker than his arm; Topper was diagramming plays with bottle caps; Alphonse was singing to himself while he planned his next prank; and Hollywood . . . well, he never met a mirror he didn't like. He was busy grooming himself to his own meticulous standards.

When Jack offered to give me some special coaching, I was glad to get away from Topper and his gang. However, as I walked to the doorway with Jack, Alphonse took a deck of cards from his bag and suggested a game of poker.

Topper, Hollywood, and the Professor quit what they were doing and sat around him. "Want to play, rookies?" Topper invited us.

If Barney had been a dog, his tail would have been thumping the floor in eagerness. Barney always had a taste for gambling—I'd seen it a little when we'd hustled games, but we'd never had enough dough before for him to really indulge his urge.

The problem was that his luck wouldn't have filled a thimble. And the other Dragons were almost licking their chops at the prospect of stripping him clean.

I hesitated, knowing I couldn't leave Barney to their tender mercies.

"You know what the hardest part of being a pro is?" Jack asked in a low voice. He didn't wait for me to answer. "Toughness."

"I'm in good shape," I said.

He tapped the side of his head. "I meant up here. You can't let other people get to you. Not that old coach, not Tops. Not anyone."

"Believe me. I got a tough hide," I said. Chinatown had seen to that.

He eased his bad leg onto the bench. "Barney's the weak spot in your armor."

"Barney's my friend," I insisted.

"The spotlight's only for one person at a time," he warned quietly.

I felt a little guilty at leaving Barney alone with the cardsharps, but I didn't see that I had a choice. "No gambling," I called to Barney, hoping that it wasn't going in one ear and out the other.

"Are you his babysitter?" Alphonse asked.

"More like my warden," Barney groused, and dismissed me with a wave of his hand. "Go peddle your papers."

Jack and I stepped into the empty gym, his voice echoed. "You know that I was really going to send the money."

"Sorry about the minister," I apologized.

"Your agents are just protecting you, kid," Jack said. "They knew I can't afford to cross a local churchman. Once we mailed the money, I comped him a couple of tickets and left him happy as a clam."

He was limping as if his leg were hurting him today. "So do you ever miss the spotlight?" I asked.

Jack sat down in the stands, extending his gimpy leg. "What if you love candy? Only you can't eat it anymore. So you do the next best thing. You run the candy store itself."

I pressed my hands together in mock piety. "Jack giveth the spotlight and Jack taketh."

Jack smirked. "I knew you were a smart boy." He started giving me some tips, but he interspersed those with his own stories from his playing days. He sounded like one tough, talented son of a gun.

Finally I asked him, "How much of that is true?"

"Does it matter, kid? All you need to know is that I'm the one who can fill your pockets with candy. And that's no lie." He glanced at his watch. "Whoa, we've been chewing the fat for a whole hour. I'm going to grab some dinner. Coming, kid?"

No matter what Jack said, I was still worried about Barney. "I got to check on my buddy."

"Barney's way too soft." Jack got awkwardly to his feet. "Don't let that softness rub off on you."

"Not a chance, with you around. You'll keep me lean and mean," I assured him sarcastically.

"It's not a joke," he snapped as he left.

Barney immediately tried to put the bite on me when I went back. "Loan me a sawbuck, Cal?" he asked. I'd already repaid him for the postcard loan.

"What happened to your allowance?" I asked, but I already knew the answer.

"Went through it," he admitted real hangdog. "So I've already had to promise to do everyone's laundry for a week. But you know me. I'll get it back."

"That's the trouble, I do. You've got the lousiest poker face," I said, shaking my head. "No dice." I'd meant I wasn't going to do it, but then I figured that someone might actually have some bones in their bag, so I added for emphasis, "No dice literally."

It looked like for the next week, my allowance was going to have to cover us both.

Barney went back to the others. "Advance me some money. I'll work it off somehow," he wheedled.

I hooked an arm through his and dragged him out of the locker room. "Come on, Mr. Poker, I'll treat you to a hamburger."

Even though we were tired from traveling and playing so many games, we won that night's game by a big score, and I made enough good plays to keep the crowd happy. It was a strange sensation to spring into the air, trying to catch a glimpse of the basket and having reporters' camera bulbs go off. There were times in that game when I almost felt like a Flash rather than a Calvin.

When we chugged into the next town, our posters were all over the streetlights and telephone poles, and fliers littered the sidewalks. "The promoter's done right by us, boys," Jack said, and slowed Annie down.

Alphonse gave a whistle. "It looks like a blizzard hit the town."

We all craned our necks to look around.

Barney lunged over the backseat and hit the horn. *A-roo-ga.*

As we rolled along slowly, I saw people turn and point. It took a moment to realize they were looking at us. We were celebrities.

"Wave, guys," Jack said.

A-roo-ga, a-roo-ga! Jack was punching the horn on his own, and Gabriel's trumpet couldn't have sounded sweeter.

When we got to the auditorium, the promoter's cigar stub bobbed up and down. "Which one of you is the human flea?" When we all looked blank, he jerked the stub from his mouth to reveal tobacco-stained teeth. "The guy with the jump gimmick."

"It's no gimmick," Topper said. "It's a real shot."

"Yeah, whatever," the promoter said. "You guys might be used to it on the West Coast, but it's new here, so that's how I puffed the show tonight."

So maybe Jack was right: The game on court—which we won handily, by the way—was just part of a bigger game.

Next we traveled on to Nevada, passing through mountains where the winds made Annie rock like a boat in a storm. And the laundry, which Barney had washed in the sink of a gas station restroom, had been hung on ropes attached to the car and was flapping like wet flags. When something purple fluttered by, I figured it was just some kind of funny-colored bird, but Hollywood pounded on the door. "Stop the car! Stop the car!"

Alphonse, who was driving, hit the brakes and looked back wildly. "Jeepers, did I hit something?"

Hollywood was already jerking the door open. "No, I just saw my shorts go by." He started to dash behind us, but by the time we all piled out of the car, he had come to a halt and was watching forlornly as his shorts drifted like a violet leaf down the face of the cliff.

"I couldn't help it," Barney wailed. "It's the cheap clothespins that Jack bought."

"Then you can buy better ones," Jack said.

"And a new pair of shorts," Topper grunted.

Hollywood pivoted and stalked back grimly to the car. "They better be purple silk."

Once out of the mountains we found ourselves in a desert that swept on and on. The sea of yellow sand and cacti was such a contrast to the lush green of the San Joaquin Valley, but after the first mile, the next two hundred got pretty boring. And when the mountains dropped below the horizon behind us, I felt like we were the last humans on the earth.

Annie could barely make twenty miles an hour with the load she was carrying so it was a long, smelly car ride. The desert at that time of the year was surprisingly cold and we had to keep the windows rolled up. We wound up arriving barely in time for the next game. It was in a converted theater in what was left of an old mining town, so we drew a mixed crowd. There were miners left idle when the mines had closed and Easterners in gaudy Hollywood cowboy outfits because the only businesses there now were dude ranches, where Easterners could pretend to be cowboys and married women stayed to wait for their divorce papers to come through. (The Professor told me it was easier to get a divorce in Nevada, but you had to stay a certain number of days first.)

From the roof down, the theater was the fanciest place I'd ever played in because it had lots of gilded cherubs (though the gilt was flaking away) and paintings on the ceiling. The chandelier had been removed, leaving a gaping hole, so the only light was cast by the brass fixtures remaining on the walls. They were all noble heroes and maidens looking down in astonishment at what had happened to their home.

All the seats had been taken out and a floor had been put in over the old sloping one, but the carpenter hadn't been good with a level, so it tilted a little. Topper made a note to try to get that end for the fourth quarter.

When we got there, there was a swing band blasting away and couples on the floorboards because there was a dance before the game, during halftime, and then afterward. Our game was just the break between shifts of the band.

The floor not only still had an incline, but the boards were waxed and slippery, made more for dancing than for a game, so the footing was treacherous. As if that wasn't bad enough, our opponent, the Miners, had a real giant— seven feet in his stockings—and as strong as an ox. His hands were so big he could have swung a pickax in each and worked a mine himself—if there were any mines open. And when he ran, the rafters shook.

He was the last guy I wanted to go up against, and after all the miles and all the games, the whole team was exhausted. We could barely run let alone jump, our passes didn't have any zip, and our shots fell short.

When it was my turn for a rest, I was glad to slump down on the bench. Jack was hunched forward, his elbows on his knees, looking like a falcon ready to dive onto his prey. "I told Topper to run the legs off these guys just like we did against the Cavaliers. Why isn't he?"

I stifled a yawn. "We're worn-out from that schedule you put together."

He jabbed me in the chest. "Then it's up to you to pick up the team." He pointed at the Giant as he plodded by. "He's laughing at you, kid. I've seen him. And so's the rest of his team. They think you're nothing."

I stiffened. "Then they don't know me."

Jack leaned over to whisper fiercely. "That's right. You show them, kid. You show them all. Anyone who's ever doubted you or insulted you."

I could feel the anger rising in me as I thought of my old man and the Guests and the insults they threw at me every chance they got. I realized by then that Jack was making up what he was saying. He was just stoking the fire already in my boiler. He kept talking to me until I felt like I was ready to explode, and then he signed to the team to call a time-out. I knew what he was doing, but it woke a passion in me anyway.

"Now go get 'em, tiger," Jack said.

The Giant was just about their whole offense, and they ran plays to isolate him on the smallest opponent. So I was expecting something the next time they had the ball.

I was covering the guard with the ball, but out of the corner of my eye, I saw the Giant plant himself a few feet to the left of the basket. I'd seen them run the play a half dozen times, so I knew the Miners were setting up a screen.

"Switch!" I shouted in warning.

I had to halt before I collided with the Giant, but the guard continued on, brushing past him toward the basket. That meant that the Professor, who was defending the big center, had to move around him to stop the guard and I had to take the Giant myself. Of course, the guard flipped the ball back to the Giant. I was then faced with the task of trying to stop a moving redwood. Only, I didn't have to—because I swiped the ball right out of his big paws.

I whirled around to go to the other basket, calling to the nearest Dragon, "Come on. Move it!"

"Don't tell me what to do, rookie," Hollywood snapped, but he began to run faster to show me he could work just as hard as me. And our teammates did the same.

I started to take the Miners apart single-handedly and goaded the other Dragons, telling them to pick it up. I kept them and the Giant constantly running back and forth mercilessly. Of course, my anger could only take me so far before it eventually ebbed; but by then the Giant was gasping for breath with his hands on his knees, unable to move from beneath his own basket.

Even then, the Giant remained a problem because all he had to do was stick up one of his huge mitts to block any shot, but since he couldn't get up off the floor, he was a patsy for my running one-handed shot.

He took his team's eventual loss in good spirits and even bought one of Topper's photographs, moving and speaking in a slow, gentle manner—as if he had grown up trying not to step on all the little people around him.

Afterward, when I was finished with the shower, I didn't wait to dry myself off. I just wrapped a towel around myself and found Jack waiting by the door, scribbling something on the back of an envelope. By the time I worked up the nerve to ask him my question, I was shivering.

"Yeah?" he asked without looking up. I saw he was adding a column of numbers.

"Before you put me in the first time, it was like . . ." I hesitated, "like you could read my mind."

"I had as much to prove when I was your age," he shrugged, "so it was easy to figure out what to say. It's going to be a long road, kid. You gotta have something to rev up your motor every game." I wasn't sure I wanted to get my motor going that way, and it was a little creepy to think I might have something in common with an old geezer like him.

"Is that what you said to yourself when you were still playing?"

"Whaddya think?" He looked like he wanted to say more, but I don't think he was used to talking about this stuff any more than I was. Finally he motioned me away. "Now scram. You're dripping on the account book."

When we found out the theater was giving away free plates later, we all wanted to stay; but Jack nixed it, saying that we had to cover three hundred miles for the next game. He passed through ghost towns to a town that seemed like it was going to become one.

But the whole town turned out because, as we found out when we had fiddled with the radio at a café, there was nothing but static to be heard. The big boxy radio was there more for decoration than for music. The moving picture show was all boarded up, so we were the only entertainment in town. Even then, there weren't enough people to fill the converted roller-skating rink, and Jack started to get worry lines on his forehead when he saw the take.

We barnstormed through Nevada, winning everywhere. I even got a few cheers when I took a running one-handed shot, as if people had come to see the new oddity.

When we had been pulling our con, Barney and I might play three or four games a day, but it was nothing like this grind. We crisscrossed the state, traveling all night to get to one town and then doubling back to play in another town in the county we had left the night before. There was a game almost every night and two games on Sundays; and after a while we were all feeling the grind of the schedule.

What got me through it all was Jack—he always had some tip from the old days or even just a pat on the back whenever I needed it—and the fact that I liked being

Flash, the star of the backboard. Sometimes it almost seemed like Flash was more real than Calvin.

However, I made sure that my passing was just as flashy as my shooting. By now, I was starting to get a feel for where the guys were going to be on a play, so I turned the ball over less and less and zipped the ball to them instead. I wound up ignoring the playbook half the time, but since I set the others up better than Topper did, the rest of the Dragons began listening to me, and when I did something special, the only one who griped out loud was Topper. Jack made a point of calling it sour grapes on Topper's part, and the other Dragons were starting to look like they agreed.

Because of my play, we also began filling the stands every night. Suddenly there were good meals and plenty of liniment and bandages, and Jack somehow managed to make it sound like it was coming from me.

And once a week, there would be some minister, priest, rabbi, or even a nun who would show up to supervise the mailing of our salary. Jack accepted his fate with good grace and humor. "I've been hounded before by bill collectors, but never by holy ones. I can't even swear at them."

There were also piles of newspapers that had stories about our games, which I assumed he mailed ahead to reporters on our schedule.

The only bad thing about having all the newspapers was that the front pages made the Professor worry more and more. Russia had invaded Finland, but Finland was kicking them in their teeth, and the Germans had a ship called the *Admiral Graf Spee* that was sailing around the Atlantic sinking British ships. He tried to use the news to convince us that the whole world was heading toward war, but the rest of us only had one thought: winning the next game.

I thought Nevada had been desert, but it was nothing compared to Utah, where the ground was flat and barren and the sun shone off it so brightly that I thought it was going to burn my eyeballs, except it was even colder. The Professor said it was the Great Salt Lake and was the white salt left over when a sea had dried up. It was pretty awe inspiring in a depressing sort of way. When we stopped to stretch our legs, I couldn't get over all the gnats that rose in clouds at each step, but near the city, I saw farms that reminded me of California. It was hard to believe they had been created out of that desert.

When we headed into Utah, Barney and me wanted to stop at Promontory Point, where the Central Pacific and Union Pacific railroads had met, linking the whole country and signaling the finish of our families' work. But Jack refused, insisting that we had to make time.

We played a game in Salt Lake City against the Bankers, where the ref must've weighed a ton and wheezed so badly that he could only manage a feeble tweet on his whistle. He made up for it by windmilling his arms—which made his blubbery body jiggle.

Mostly we played in little towns against teams named the Spuds or the Plumbers and other odd names—everything but the candlestick makers. And as we drove along, I could see how lucky we were. The towns were clean enough—though there were plenty of stores boarded up, but it was the Okies that got me. You could see them chugging westward. I wanted to shout at them that California was no paradise, but I don't think they would have believed me. The Professor said that everyone needed hope. But no one would hire those guys any more than they'd hire Chinese.

Sometimes they'd be broken down by the road and just sit there all hangdog, looking ready to die. Or you'd pass by camps that were full of so many old rusty rattletraps that they looked more like junkyards than camps for people. Things were bad in San Francisco, with plenty of folks sleeping on the streets and begging, but it was nothing like what I was seeing in the rest of the country.

Hollywood unwrapped a stick of gum and popped it in his mouth. "You know those newsreels about the war in China? All those refugees running from the Japanese? Well, it looks like there's a war on in Oklahoma and all these folks are on the run."

"Except the Okies have got cars—and I use the term loosely," Jack said, steering Annie around yet another broken-down heap.

The contrast between them and us got even stronger the night we stayed in a hotel for the first time. Jack got some kind of sweetheart deal with the local promoter who owned the place. We had dinner in the hotel restaurant— pork chops a couple of inches thick and stuffed with dressing and all the apple pie á la mode we could eat.

Though we all had to share the same room, Barney and I got a bed because when we cut cards I took our turn and won. I felt like a king when I slipped under clean sheets for the first time in . . . well, I couldn't remember when I'd ever gotten to sleep between sheets.

That night, as the laundry dried over the steam radiator and water drops hissed against the hot metal, Barney sat down to write his postcard to Tiger about the high life we were leading.

I'd had it beaten into my head not to count on good stuff because it'd been my experience that you never get to keep it for long. Sometimes when Dad was having the D.T.'s, he'd talk about demons all around him trying to snatch at our stuff. There were times when I thought those demons might be real, like they were dogging me as well, that bragging about my success would just make them take it away all the faster.

"You're going to jinx it," I warned.

Barney wrinkled his forehead in thought, acting as if he were writing a sonnet rather than a postcard. "I want to share this with Tiger since she can't be here in person."

I thought guiltily of how Jean would have liked to stay in a hotel instead of sharing a bed with two sisters. I still had a few blank postcards, but I couldn't get past the salutation. I was lousy with words, even if I'd known what to say.

I wound up taking out one of my prewritten postcards and found a line I had already scribbled that said, *Wish you were here* and squeezed in a *really* at the beginning. I paused and then underlined it for emphasis. Still, that didn't seem enough. So I added *Your Chum* just above my signature.

As I stuck a stamp on it, I hoped she'd understand and forgive. Then I took it down to the mailbox and sent her fee on the way.

CHAPTER | XI

Annie rattled on into Idaho where we saw the first snow in our lives. Spoilsport Jack didn't want to stop because he said he'd shoveled more snow than he ever wanted to, but we made such a racket that he finally screeched to a stop—the car fishtailing on the icy road. He sat in the car and glowered while we clambered out. "No play, no pay," he groused from the jalopy, "so don't break a leg."

We were all too excited to care. The snow was so cold and fluffy and melted on our hands.

When he saw what we were doing, Jack tore his hair—and he didn't have a lot to begin with. "Don't get your fingers frostbit for heaven's sake!"

Alphonse started belting out "Winter Wonderland" and then threw himself in the snow like he'd seen someone do in a movie once, showing the rest of us how to make angels.

That made Killjoy Jack shout at us that we'd get colds doing a stupid stunt like that.

I forget who threw the first snowball—probably Alphonse—but in no time we were flinging handfuls of the stuff at one another. That was just too much for the meticulous Jack to bear. He forgot all about schedules and money woes.

"No, no, no, Flash!" he said, finally getting out of his mobile fortress. "You're not packing the snowballs tight enough." He shuffled in small steps toward us, not even pausing as he scooped up some snow, shaped it into a ball, and whipped it at Topper with a sideways motion. "Like that."

The next instant, we were all making snowballs that really threw well, and we kept at it until we were out of breath.

Jack drew the line, though, about letting us build a big snowman because it would take too much time. But he did let us build a small one out of some leftover snowballs.

I have to admit that, as we jounced our way back and forth across the state, the snow's appeal wore off quicker than Annie's cheap paint job. The snow turned quickly to ugly, dirty slush that made roads slick and travel slow. No matter how many layers of clothing we wore, we couldn't seem to keep warm.

Most of the time we slept in the car as we traveled to the next game; but when the schedule allowed, we stayed at Ys or skid-row dives where the walls were paper thin, the bedbugs outnumbered us, and the hot water in the shower never lasted longer than five seconds.

Still, it was nice to be in them and escape winter for a while and after a particularly cold stretch where we were feeling like icicles, we welcomed staying in a YMCA. However, once we'd thawed out, it didn't take long before we felt trapped by the darkness and the cold and the snow, so the team started to play poker. But I nixed that idea and hauled Barney out into the hallway when he tried to join in. "They'd skin us alive," I argued. "They've probably got some code of hidden signals to one another."

Sometimes Barney could be as innocent as the newly fallen snow. "They're our teammates, Cal. They'd never cheat us."

"Your problem is that you trust everyone," I said.

Barney looked me straight in the eye. "And your problem is that you don't trust enough."

So there was no choice but to handcuff myself to Barney and make sure that he could only watch forlornly as the others played.

Keeping one eye on my pal, I took out a blank postcard. The room's steam radiator hissed and clanked and made the place feel like a sweatbox.

I wanted to tell Jean that I'd seen my first snow, but then all that blank space seemed to invite more words, so I began to ask about home. Was Johnny Kan still baking those little loaves? Were they still holding the parades for the war? The words came pouring out of me so I had to use another postcard, and by the time I wrote on a third, I realized I was homesick. I missed Chinatown. And most of all, I missed Jean.

We soon got to hate the snow as much as Jack did. With the weather turning miserable, people began to stay at home rather than come out to see us. Houses started to get small again and traveling became hard. There were times when Annie could only inch along while the driver hunched forward, trying to see through the falling snow.

Our clothes were all starting to smell because it was hard to do our laundry unless the newspaper predicted a thaw that day. Then we could hang the laundry outside the car on ropes again. A couple of times our clothes froze on the lines, and the car looked like it was surrounded by starched invisible men, but then the sun came out and our clothes finally dried—to everyone's relief but Hollywood's most of all. He hated to look sloppy.

What I really hated was the ice. When the snow thawed a little, it would melt, and when it froze again, it turned to ice and often got hidden by a new snowfall. We skidded on one patch and overturned, but Annie—for all her age and her complaints—was built like a tank. We dug her out of the snow, warming our frozen, aching fingers in our armpits—which is a trick Barney had heard about from Grandpa Joe. Then we righted her and saw she just had a few dings.

Somehow, despite the snow, we made every game, taking on more local teams with names like the Grocers or the Bartenders and winning most of them—though what I remember were the losses, especially a particular one where we had played in a huge armory that felt as cold as outside. For some reason, there were no bleachers, just benches right near the sides, and the crowd was all bundled up.

The ref had tried to help out the home team, the Cooks, by calling fouls on just us, so we taught him a lesson like we had the ref in the Bakers game.

However, after he stopped calling fouls, the fans decided to lend a hand. When I tried to inbound a ball, I felt a sharp pain in my behind. I gave a jump and when I turned, I saw a lady tucking away a wicked-looking hat pin. Or we might be running down the court when caps from beer bottles were tossed at us or a lit cigarette would flick out of the crowd and burn one of us. Somebody even threw a lit cigar at Hollywood, barely missing his photogenic cheek. "And it was a cheap cigar too," he said, putting a hand protectively on his face.

Things like that—sometimes relatively harmless, sometimes outright dangerous—happened wherever we played. It would have been nice to be the home team for once. Sure, the crowd wound up cheering for us sometimes, but it took so much work to win them over.

Still, I understood that whenever people booed us during a game, it was because we were beating their family and friends. Heck, I would have done the same. Kellogg, Idaho, though, was a different kettle of fish.

The evergreen trees on the hills around Kellogg stood like vampires watching us as we chugged past, and I couldn't shake off an uneasy feeling.

I didn't feel any better when we checked in with the promoter because the first thing he did was reassure us, "Now, I don't want you boys to fret. The sheriff's not going to throw you into the hoosegow. You're perfectly safe."

"We haven't done anything wrong," Topper protested. We couldn't have even gotten a speeding ticket because of Annie's asthmatic engine. At most, they could fine us for being seen in a public eyesore.

"But we got a law on the books hereabouts: No Chinese allowed in the city. It's been on the books for almost sixty years," the promoter explained. "But the sheriff said that seeing as how you're just passing through, it's no problem."

I worked out the math and realized sixty years ago was the depths of the anti-Chinese craziness, when mobs had burnt down whole Chinatowns and killed anyone who had the wrong skin color. Suddenly I thought of all the horror stories that I'd heard about those days. "It's a long time to nurse a grudge."

The promoter shrugged. "We got long memories, but the ones who really got to worry are these boys." He pointed to a stack of posters scattered in one corner of his office on the floor. They were torn and defaced, and rude words had been scrawled on them—the words often misspelled. At least I thought they had been defaced, but then I saw they had beards and hair down to their waists. "I can't keep their posters up," the promoter said.

"The House of David," I read. That was the team we were going to play that night. "Are they Jewish?"

"No, they come from some Christian group up in Michigan," the promoter said. "They're always a good draw, but there's a few folks object to their looks."

Jack was shaking his head at me as a signal to keep my trap shut, but I couldn't resist griping, "If folks passed a law like that, there were more than just a few who objected to our mugs too."

The promoter just grinned. "That's why you're such good business. There's some folks who want to see two good teams go at it. And then there'll be other folks who want to see the longhairs get beat. And the rest'll be there to see you China boys get stomped. I've sold most of the tickets already."

"There's no moss growing on you," Jack said, glad to hear that the house was sold out.

Jack usually had some tips for me before every game, but I'd never seen him look so concerned before. "This is the first time you go up against real professionals, so just be careful. They've got some ringers—guys who don't belong to their faith but are real good at the game."

But after so many wins I was feeling awfully confident. Thanks to Jack's lessons, I'd learned to sleep okay in the car, and my legs were feeling fresh enough to outhop a jackrabbit. "Those old geezers?" I laughed. "They've got to be over thirty if they're a day."

Jack frowned. "Those old 'geezers' have played more real games in a year than you have in your life. When they aren't touring the country as a basketball team, they tour it as a baseball team."

I shed my jacket and tossed it on the bench. "Then they're all worn-out."

"Some guys gotta learn the hard way," Jack groused.

I strutted out on the court, feeling like Flash more than ever, and took my place for the tip-off.

The Professor was three inches shorter than their center, but he timed his jump perfectly and slapped the ball to me.

I broke for the basket, and though one of the geezers planted himself right underneath it, I figured that ton of hair and beard would make him so top heavy that he couldn't hop high enough to block my running one-handed shot.

But he went up like he had rockets for legs, up and up, and he swatted that ball away. When he landed, he glared at me as if there was no way he was ever going to let me make a basket.

"Flash, get back!" Topper shouted.

I turned to see that he had batted the ball to a guard who had so much hair that he looked like a blond shrub. Topper had said he was the team's manager, and he was a lefty. Sneakers squeaking, I pivoted to run when Rocket Man knocked me from behind. I skidded across the floor, peeling off a layer of skin, and watched his high-tops disappear downcourt.

Because of their size, the Davids liked to toss the ball to their big men when they were close to the basket. And try as we might, we couldn't stop them from scoring because they were as experienced and athletic as we were—and even bigger. And if they missed, they usually beat us to the rebound.

Still, I finally managed to get a rebound, so the Shrub darted over to guard me, balancing on the balls of his feet and darting from side to side. I faked a pass to my left and he moved in that direction. Then I bounce-passed the ball under his outstretched hand to Topper.

Topper signaled a play to the rest of the Dragons and then tossed it back to me. But as he ran ahead with the others, the Shrub cut in front of me. I didn't have to see the other David that came up behind me because I could smell his sweaty, hairy hide and hear his sneakers.

Suddenly I was trapped in a David sandwich. No matter where I pivoted, there seemed to be some huge

mitt waving in front of me. I couldn't see a Dragon anywhere. Other teams had tried this against me, but they
weren't as quick as the Davids, who seemed to anticipate
my every move. The next thing I knew, the ref was blowing his whistle because I had traveled.

As the Shrub inbounded the ball, Topper came over
and whispered to me, "Settle down, kid."

"It was a fluke," I insisted. Sure it was—as much of a
rarity as when I lost the ball a second and a third time.

As soon as I had the ball, two and even three Davids
converged on me. That meant there was a Dragon left
free, but I couldn't get the ball to him if I couldn't see
him. And even when I did manage to pass it to a Dragon,
the Davids played sharp defense, switching easily from
playing us man to man to zones where each of them
would take an area of the court. It was my job to recognize the defense, but they were good at disguising what
they were doing.

I wound up getting more and more rattled until I
dribbled the ball off my foot.

"Time!" Jack shouted, and sent Barney in.

As I sat down, ashamed, on the bench, I draped a
towel over my head. "I know, I know. You told me they
were good."

"You're not going to be able to outjump, out-quick,
or out-tall them." Jack lifted the edge of the towel so he
could whisper in my ear. "So what's left?"

I was grateful Jack was on my side. "Hunh . . . out-think?"

Jack tapped the side of his head. "No matter how mad or scared you get, the gears in your brain should always be turning. So what happened?"

I felt like it was the next step I had to master. Suddenly I slapped my head. It was plain as the nose on my face, but I'd been so rattled that I hadn't seen it. "They're doing to me what I did to that kid from the Windmills."

Jack patted me on the shoulder. "They played you for a sap, but they can't keep up this pace for the whole game. Once you show them that they can't upset you, they'll quit."

When I went back in and got the ball again, I almost panicked when the Davids surrounded me. But I told myself to calm down. I pretended to stare at a spot as if there were a Dragon there. One of them moved his hands to block my throw while the other tried to slap the ball from my hands—but too late. I'd already lobbed the ball over them to where Hollywood would be running on that play.

And suddenly instead of facing a hairy wall, I was in the open as the Davids turned and ran back to help on defense. But it was already too late because Hollywood was banking an easy shot into the basket. The Davids tried to trap me a few more times, but I just did what we had already practiced in San Francisco. After we made them pay after each try, they gave up.

And Hollywood was hot, shooting from beyond the Davids' defense, so I made sure to get the ball to him when I didn't have a shot. Everything we threw up seemed to come down with that sweet swish through the net. The Davids had no choice but to come out to meet us, which opened up the inside so I could either drive or pass to an open Dragon. By the end of the second quarter, we were leading by seven.

When the referee blew his whistle for intermission, the manager for the House of David sidled over to me. Like Topper, he played as well as acted as coach. "Bless you, brother. Good game," he said piously.

"I haven't had this much fun in a long time," I agreed.

He dropped his voice. "But I'm concerned for your soul, brother. Vanity is a deadly sin. You shouldn't put on such vainglorious displays."

"As I recall, your team's been hawking the ball from me," I said. "Isn't stealing another sin?"

He clicked his tongue. "But we are only doing the Lord's work. Everything we earn goes to our church. We play to pray. And what will we do if you beat us? Have mercy, brother."

And I thought of what basketball meant to me. "Well, I pray to play." I moved away from him. "And I'm no one's brother."

"What were you talking about?" Barney asked as he drank some tea.

"How too much fun is bad for you," I laughed.

Barney scratched his head as he looked over at their

bench. "I didn't think they were ministers too."

No, they were prophets, good at fulfilling their own predictions.

I should have known that they were setting me up when we got the tip-off too easy. I couldn't believe the clear highway I had to the basket, but as I started to streak toward it, from the corner of my eye I saw someone darting toward me. And then I was flying literally toward a wall. I bounced off and clunked my head hard on the floorboards. In a cartoon, I would have been seeing little birdies fluttering overhead.

I dimly heard the ref blowing his whistle. As I lay there, I saw Alphonse lean over, his head seeming to float above me like a cloud. "You okay, Flash?"

I shut my eyes for a moment. I could almost imagine hearing my father laugh that he had told me so: I was going to get myself killed. Who knew he'd predicted the truth for once?

I guess I was punch-drunk like a boxer who'd taken one to the head, because I began to giggle.

I heard Alphonse shouting. "There's something wrong with Flash."

If I was going to die, I might as well do it upright, so I raised my arm. "I'm okay, but help me up."

Because I felt as if the world was still swimming around me, I kept my eyes closed as he lifted me to my feet.

Suddenly a whistle blew shrilly. "That's a technical," the ref yelled.

I opened my eyes. The world was stable again, more or less, and I saw the referee pointing at Jack.

Jack was beyond caring. "That thug just mugged my boy. He ought to get thrown out."

The referee raised his index finger in warning. "You give me any more lip, and you're the one who's going to get the bum's rush."

Jack got as red as a boiled crab, and the tendons stood out on his neck. "What's wrong with you?"

Fortunately, Topper and Hollywood grabbed him and pulled him away, but he shouted complaints all the way to the bench.

Alphonse shook his head in wonder. "I've never seen Jack so worked up. As soon as he saw what they did to you, he came charging onto the court, wanting the ref to eject that David."

"All this fresh air must be making him funny in the head," I said. I told myself he was just keeping his part of the bargain to take care of me . . . and yet you don't get this angry when you're protecting a business investment. Just what was Jack's game now?

The David's manager was grinning from ear to ear as he shot the technical foul and got another point for his team.

And then the referee turned to me. "You all right?"

"Yeah." I held out my hands for the ball.

When I walked to the foul line, I called to the David's manager, who crouched with arms already spread out to stop my teammates, "Thanks for the lesson." When I sank the foul shot, I said, "I owe you."

And on the way to the tip-off, I fixed my eyes on him as if he had an invisible bull's-eye.

During the tip-off, the Professor was unusually clumsy—maybe he was tired, but he actually tapped the ball to the manager. As he was driving to the basket, Hollywood threw a crushing block on him that sent him sprawling and the ball rolling straight to Topper, who lobbed it to me. It was an easy drive to the basket and two more points—that didn't count, of course, because it was after a foul. The poor referee turned blue blowing his whistle as if he were auditioning to be a factory siren. When I came down, I saw Topper and the other Dragons fronting the Davids.

"And that's payback," Topper warned. "Now we can get into a brawl." My teammates nodded their heads in agreement. "But," Topper went on smoothly, "how's that going to look for your image?"

The manager dusted off his rear. He beamed as saintly as he could as he pressed his hands together in mock prayer. "Heaven forbid."

As we took our positions again, I asked Topper, "Why'd you do that? It's between him and me."

"Whether you like it or not, it's 'us' against 'them,'" Topper grunted. "We may not like you, but the only ones who can pick on you is us."

After that little incident, my education didn't stop in the second half, but the lessons weren't nearly so brutal (except to my pride). The Davids' manager knew a hundred ways to trick an opponent, some of which left me on the floor. I just picked myself up and filed away his little lessons for my own use.

I don't know what sparked the other Dragons—maybe it was my run-in with the Davids' manager or maybe it was something else—but they all put their game into high gear. We put on a press of our own and got our own share of steals. Somehow tired legs raced and jumped, and when there was a rebound, three Dragons in red uniforms suddenly materialized around it while Topper and I raced toward the other basket, ready for their pass.

I wouldn't have told Topper, but this was the first game that I was glad I was with the other Dragons—because there was no way I wanted to lose to the Davids.

I no longer felt alone out there on the floor. I could depend on them as much as I could on Barney. There were even special moments when I felt as if there were some invisible cord connecting each of us: In those wonderful seconds, we were a living thing rather than Topper's machine.

We even wound up winning—though not by as big a margin as I would have liked. "I don't make the same mistake twice," I said to Jack as I shuffled toward the car. "I won't lose my head again."

He just grinned. "You're learning, kid."

I tried to hoist my bag to my shoulder, but I ached too much. "One thing, though: You said to play it smart, and yet you lost your temper and got called for a technical."

He shrugged, embarrassed. "You got talent, kid. I don't want to see your career get cut short by some thug."

I was always suspicious of people who offered to do me favors out of the kindness of their hearts. "So were you just protecting your investment?" Even though I told myself I was being an idiot, I found myself desperately wanting to believe he'd been doing more.

He looked at me, hurt, and opened his mouth but shut it again as if he thought better of it. Then the smirk snapped back in place. "Sure, that's old Jack: Got a cash box where my heart ought to be."

And he limped away.

CHAPTER | XII

T he other games in Idaho weren't as rough as the game against the House of David, but we were all pretty worn-out by the time we headed on to the next state. Jack not only had bags under his eyes from lack of sleep, but he was constantly worrying about money now because the audiences were so small. It was so cold folks didn't want to leave their snug little homes.

One farm town played that same keepaway-style that the Windmills had used; but without an Old Fox to coach them, we had no problem beating them. The fans, though, were another problem. They were real hooligans, so the biggest excitement in the game came when Topper was speeding down the court with Hollywood and Barney on either side for the basket—when all of a sudden a fan jumped out of the stands and belted Topper.

As soon as the ref tried to throw the fan out, someone else threw a beer bottle that hit him square in the nose. The ref stood there for a moment with blood streaming from his schnozola onto his shirt and then set an Olympic record dashing for the exit.

At the time that happened, I was sitting on the bench with Jack. I looked around at the crowd that was getting nastier by the second. The timekeeper—as well as the rest of the Dragons—was eyeing the door as if ready to follow the ref to safety too. For that matter, I was getting pretty jittery myself.

Jack just set his jaw, though. "Never show animals that you're scared, kid," he muttered to me as he stripped off his suit coat.

"What're you doing?" I asked, mystified.

"I'm going to show them what it means to be a pro," he said, rolling up his shirtsleeves.

As I watched him limp onto the court, I couldn't decide if he was either the bravest or dumbest man I'd ever met.

"I'll ref," he announced.

"Are you crazy?" Alphonse asked.

"We got paid to play, so we play." Jack gave a jerk when another beer bottle sailed out of the stands and thumped him in the back. He turned calmly, studied the liquid spilling from the mouth of the bottle and picked it up. "You ought to be ashamed of yourselves," he shouted to the mob. "Someone's thrown away a perfectly good beer." The gym suddenly got quiet as he tilted back his head and swigged it down as if he were in his favorite bar surrounded by his cronies. When he'd emptied the bottle, he belched and then called, "Now do you want a game, or do you want to go on wasting your beer?"

The crowd roared their approval and Jack set the bottle on the sidelines. When he held up his hand, I tossed him a towel so he could wipe up the puddle.

Jack didn't stop those hoodlums from throwing things, but at least there were no more beer bottles or punches. And I have to say Jack was a fairer ref than most, even if he had trouble running on his bum leg.

We were all grateful to escape with a win as well as our skins so we piled into Annie for the all-night drive to the next town.

"Why'd you do that?" I asked Jack. "Were you afraid of not getting paid?"

Jack chuckled. "We didn't even break even, kid."

"Then why didn't you just take a powder?" I asked, puzzled.

"Because there's more to winning than just the scoreboard," he said.

A couple of hours past midnight, it got so cold that any thermometer would have frozen. We had some of the newspapers to wrap around us under our shirts for extra insulation. Jack kept out the sports page, and the Professor retained the news section so he could read by moonlight about the wars around the world. "The Chinese are winning," he informed us.

"They're always winning, but somehow the Japanese always take more and more of the country," Topper grunted skeptically.

The Professor told us that the Russians were finally grinding down the poor Finns, who just didn't have the bench, as he put it, and the British had trapped the *Admiral Graf Spee* in Uruguay and the German captain had scuttled it.

"I don't know where Uruguay is," Hollywood yawned, "and I don't care."

"It's warm," Alphonse informed him, "so I wish I was there."

"Don't worry," Topper said. "Jack's trying to set up a game there next week."

It wouldn't have surprised any of us, because after so many miles, we'd given up asking where we were heading, so the next morning it was a rude shock when I saw the battered, faded sign saying: WELCOME TO WYOMING.

I straightened immediately. "Did you see?" I asked Barney.

Barney nodded and then just stared out the window quietly.

"See what?" Hollywood asked. He looked at the snowy land rolling past us. "Wyoming looks a lot like Idaho."

Barney didn't seem to want to talk, so I told the others a little about what Grandpa Joe had told us. In a coal-mining town called Rock Springs, striking miners had massacred the Chinese miners who had tried to replace them. Grandpa Joe and his father had only escaped because two white friends had hidden them from the mob. I don't think the landscape had changed any since he'd been here fifty years or so ago.

Jack was in the back to take a nap. He stretched as best as he could without hitting someone. "No kidding. How come I never heard about that?"

"It's not something that gets into the history books," the Professor said. The rest of the team was sitting silently because they had heard the stories too.

"Well, it's not going to happen now. It's 1939, for heaven's sake," Jack snapped.

"Where are we playing?" Barney asked anxiously.

"Rock Springs," Jack grunted.

We were all tense when we rolled into town. I half expected to see a mob with torches and tar and feathers, but there was just the usual gawking and finger-pointing (the surprised kind, not the pantomime guns). The little hotel didn't make a fuss when we walked into the lobby—they only cared about the color of our money and not our skin—and the waitress at the diner said that we reminded her of her sons, so she not only gave us extra biscuits and gravy but even boiled our tea for the game.

There was some booing, but no more than in other places, and by the end we had the place cheering our good plays. "Maybe they've forgotten too," I said to Barney.

"Let's hope so," Barney said.

Jack had overheard us. The house had been good, and he was feeling more confident now. "Why wouldn't they?" he assured us. "The massacre isn't anything you want your grandkids to know. It's a clean slate, boys. So cheer up. Besides, you're not a threat to their livelihoods. You're entertainers passing through town." He held out his hand. "And don't hog the tea."

So he, Barney, and I were the only ones who didn't get sick. It was a quick bug that lasted for only twenty-four hours, but for the next game it left the rest of the team waddling back and forth with one eye on the door to the restroom. If we hadn't been playing yet another team of stiffs, we would have lost. As it was, we beat them only by one basket—which had them cheering as if they'd won the game. After that, the whole team began drinking tea rather than the local water.

I figured we owed Grandpa Joe, but when I tried to write him, Barney surprised me. "Ixnay on the etterlay. If you tell him that," he said, "there'll be no living with him when we go home."

I felt a little pang at the mention of Chinatown, but I also felt a little scared because going back to Chinatown was the end of the fun.

"He's going to fling pearls of wisdom at us whether we want it or not." I shrugged and wrote him a postcard. When I realized it would have a Wyoming postmark, I added a postscript, assuring him that so far most everyone had treated us just fine.

The rest of the games on the tour were like games in the other states, and we won a lot more than we lost—though every loss stung. But the weather stayed bad and the audiences small. Jack was so worried about money that one evening he kept right on driving past the fleabag hotel where we had a reservation and didn't stop until he saw an empty shack near a farmer's potato field. "This is where we'll be sleeping tonight, boys."

"In this freezing weather?" Topper asked, outraged.

Jack eyed him, ready to go toe-to-toe. "It's the lousy weather that's keeping folks at home. We barely filled a quarter of the seats that last game. So it's either the hotel or walking to the next game because we don't have gas."

The Dragons were looking rebellious so I tried to play peacemaker yet again. Next to the shack was a water tap wrapped in rags. When I turned the handle, water splashed onto the snow, starting to melt it. "Hey, look! Water wouldn't flow if it was freezing."

Jack glanced at me gratefully and then stomped his foot. "The ground's not frozen either."

"You guys ought to be writing for the funny papers," Alphonse groused. Wrapping his arms around himself for warmth, he shuffled into the shack. And one by one, our teammates followed him in there until Topper was left with just Jack, Barney, and me.

Topper shot a venomous look at me. "It must be nice being Jack's pet." But he went inside the shack too.

Barney wound up with yet another chore of picking up any dead wood lying around, but it was a bad sign that even the good-tempered Barney was muttering sullenly, echoing the Dragons in the shack.

Jack built a fire before the doorway around which we all huddled. "See. It's just like camping."

"Gee, and me with no marshmallows," Hollywood said sarcastically. It marked the start of a long evening of the Dragons grumbling out loud.

Our tempers were all foul the next game and we took it out on the other team, running up the score. Well, exercise was the only way to keep from freezing because the gym's furnace had broken down. The few fans in the stands must have been part polar bear.

I hadn't realized just how rotten things were until a few days later on Christmas Eve. We were all looking forward to getting our salary, and the town's local priest had shown up to send Barney and my salaries back to our agents. Jack had taken him off to the side. I could see both of them getting more and more frustrated as they argued. Finally, the priest announced, "Mr. Young is going to be very disappointed."

"He'll just have to get in line, Father," Jack grunted.

As the priest stalked away, Jack came over to tell us there was no money for our wages.

The Dragons exploded, spewing out a long list of grievances—everything from his being cheap to being a liar and thief. According to their venom, he'd committed every crime except blowing up the *Hindenburg* dirigible.

Jack folded his arms patiently while the others had their say until they started to repeat his sins over again like a broken record. "Look," he finally said, "I wish I could pay you what you boys deserve, but I can't control the weather. And it's not just the budget that makes us sleep in Ys. The good hotels won't take us. And neither will good restaurants. They don't serve Chinese, Negroes, or Okies."

"See, guys," I coaxed the others. "We met up with that in California on our own."

"Yeah, yeah," Jack nodded, irritated. "There's still places in this country where an Irishman can't go either." He stuck out his hand toward Topper. "We're all in the same boat together."

Topper, though, just glared at it. "We're not going to put up with much more, Jack."

"Take his hand," I urged. "We're teammates." I turned to Barney for support. "Right?"

"I'm with Tops," Barney grunted. It was the first time we'd ever really disagreed on anything, and that hurt.

The team was still looking daggers at Jack when we rolled into South Dakota the next morning. I just tried to ignore them. All I wanted for Christmas was some peace and quiet from the bickering.

By this point in the trip, I didn't pay attention to the identity of our opponents, even when Jack said we were going to play another professional team—but not to worry because they weren't the same caliber as the House of David.

Their posters in town certainly weren't as flashy as ours because they had no pictures, only words. Most of the town was shut up tight, and there hadn't been much money for decorating anyway. Here and there, some house had a Christmas tree with lights—I guess they were this dump's equivalent of the Rockefellers.

The town was so dark that the diner's lights shone out like beacons on the street. We pooled our money so we could have a Christmas meal of sorts. We were all as eager for the warmth as we were for the food as we shuffled through the snow and went inside.

Instantly, the diner fell silent; we could hear the big radio in the corner playing "Winter Wonderland." The customers all turned to stare at us just as the trophy heads on the walls were doing.

The cook was behind the counter, and I hoped his food was more sanitary than his grease-spattered clothes. "Hey," he glared, "can't you read?" He pointed at the sign over the cash register that had a small Christmas wreath and the words NO INDIANS. I guess that was another group to be added to the not-welcome list at restaurants and hotels.

"Didn't you read the posters around town?" Jack asked, annoyed. "They're the Chinese team."

The cook narrowed his little piggy eyes. "They look Indian."

With the politest smile, Topper called him a horrible name in Chinese and continued on swearing, thoroughly covering the cook's animal ancestry and whatever miserable country had spawned him.

A guy in a baseball cap and vest must have passed for the local Einstein because everyone, including the cook, turned to him. "Well," he finally announced solemnly, "I hear Chinese is singsong like that, and it don't sound like no Indian I've heard in these parts."

"But what'd you say?" the cook asked.

"It was a traditional Chinese greeting," Topper said.

The other customers relaxed after that but continued to watch us now as curiosities while the cook waved us over to some tables. Our Christmas entertainment was provided by a static-filled broadcast of Guy Lombardo and His Royal Canadians and our Christmas dinner was as greasy and unappetizing as the cook was and probably one step away from ptomaine—but it was a point of honor to eat there after our little victory. Still, we were all eager to put in our money and leave when the check came.

I thought that night's game here was going to be interesting, but I didn't know how interesting. The first thing I knew, we left the town and chugged our way over a snowy road past a huge sign welcoming us to the reservation. The game was going to be inside an auditorium next to a one-room schoolhouse and some kind of administrative building.

Barney was too busy lugging our gear into the auditorium and I was too occupied boiling the water to pay attention to anything else.

So I was surprised when I stepped out on the court to warm up and saw that the other team had black hair, brown eyes, and the same skin color as me.

"We playing Asians?" Alphonse wondered.

"No, Native Americans," the Professor said, and nodded to the name on a poster. "Or Indians as that diner's customers would call them."[1]

I guess I was just used to movie Indians, or rather Native Americans, who were in feathered warbonnets and had paint all over their faces and waving tomahawks in the air. Then I gave a start when I saw them staring just as hard at us. I guess they were used to movie Chinese with pigtails.

"A whole team of Jim Thorpes," Hollywood said with a whistle. "We're in for a game." Jim Thorpe was the

[1]The Native Americans was the name of a basketball team on an actual poster from this period.

Native American who was a super football player, but he had excelled at any sport he tried, winning at track in the Olympics.

"The crowd too," Alphonse said, nodding at the bleachers. With the game on the Reservation, the benches were full of Native Americans.

To our relief, most of our opponents weren't Jim Thorpes, but they were good and they played the game at the same fast tempo we did. It was like going up against our mirror image and that made it tough.

Their best player was a guard who was just as deadeye a shot as me, and every time he made a good play he'd kiss the jasper rings on his right hand, one for each finger. They were big rings too, so it was a wonder he could lift his hand. And he moved like a whirlwind, so I expected to see his sneakers leave scorch marks on the floorboards. Still, I figured I could outplay a raw kid like him.

However, there came a time when they had the ball, and the Native American forward had set himself up as a screen, and the Ring Man started toward his teammate. I should have switched with one of my teammates, but I wanted to show the Ring Man I was just as determined as him.

Turning sideways and putting on a burst of speed, I managed somehow to shoehorn myself between the forward and the Ring Man and keep pace with him. Then with an extra spurt of energy I not only cut off his drive but batted the ball away from him and over to Barney to set up a fast break to the basket.

Some of the white townsfolk, including the cook, had come to the game, and as I went in for a layup, I heard a roar from them. "Way to go, Chinky-chink," the cook hollered.

The cook and his gang began rooting loudly for us to beat the Native Americans. But it was praise I could have done without because they said a lot of worse things—without even realizing they were being insulting rather than encouraging. I'd been wishing we could be the home team for once, but I wasn't sure I wanted it this way.

Their cheers, though, just made Ring Man more determined to beat us, and he began to concentrate better. I thought about what had happened in the diner, the NO INDIANS sign, and I realized I'd be mad too.

As Jack had taught me, I played angry when I wanted to show the world that I wasn't gutter trash, but my fury was a baby's tantrum compared to Ring Man's. I kept waiting for his rage to ebb like mine always had, but his never did. It was as if he were at war with the whole world, and it gave him a fuel with enough octane to power a racing airplane. I never thought I'd meet someone who was madder at the world than me. Did he have an old man as mean as mine?

Halfway through the first quarter, we all knew we'd run straight into a regular buzz saw. I lost track of the number of times that the lead changed hands.

Finally, while I was on the bench taking a breather, Topper slapped the ball from their center's hands. Ring Man dove for it like his life depended on it and plowed straight into Jack.

Jack caught him before he plunged past us into the bleachers. "Easy there, Geronimo."

Ring Man shoved him away. "That's not my name," he snapped. That was fair enough, but then he punctuated his sentence by spitting on Jack.

Jack didn't pay any attention when Topper inbounded the ball. He was too busy staring at the spittle dripping down his shirt. "Take him out," he growled to me.

We were so well-matched that I had my doubts. "I'll try," I said, "but I think it'll be a toss-up on which of us will foul out first."

"Not if you get him tossed out," Jack growled. "He's close to exploding right now. Pull any dirty stunt you want, but just be sure the ref doesn't see you. Do whatever it takes. Hurt him if you have to."

I remembered what the Windmills old coach had said to me about not being a thug. "Who cares what happens in some Podunk town, Jack? If you're mad about your shirt, I'll wash it for you."

"It's not the shirt, kid." He narrowed his eyes. "I don't take guff from anyone."

I'd done a lot of things that I wasn't proud of, but I'd never set out to hurt another human being physically. "Why don't I just spit on him? Then you'd be square."

"I want him out," Jack insisted.

So, instead I tried to upset Ring Man with insults like I had that young Windmills guard, but he just threw them right back at me because he'd already heard plenty of them growing up in that town. All the while I could feel Jack's eyes boring holes into my back, waiting for me to do what he'd commanded.

In desperation, I began pulling those dirty little stunts that I'd learned, but Ring Man gave as good as he got, so we matched each other foul for foul.

Somehow, though, with a minute left, we had managed to get ahead of the Native Americans by a point. When Jack called a time-out, we were all glad for the chance to catch our breath. "Go into a stall," he ordered everyone.

I glanced at Topper, who was the coach after all. He was too winded to speak, so he just nodded. We'd done that before in other games when we'd gotten a lead of a few points. One of the new rules had added a stripe dividing the court in half, and you had ten seconds to get the ball over the line, but after that, I'd be free to just throw it around and dribble to my heart's content.

As the ref waved us back onto the court, Jack grabbed my arm. "I told you to take out Geronimo."

"But we don't need to," I protested. "We're winning."

"You got to be a battler if you want to keep the spotlight." He folded his arms across his chest. "Maybe I should get him and not you."

That hurt because I was giving 100 percent on everything else, and I almost called his bluff and told him to go ahead. But I stopped because I was scared Jack just might do it.

When we started again, they went into a full-court press, and Ring Man plastered himself to me as tight as my own sweaty uniform.

"I'll show you," he snarled. "I'll show all of you." He jerked his head toward the audience. "I won't lose to a dirty cheat like you."

Everywhere I looked he seemed to have a hand, but fortunately Hollywood got away from his man. I bounce-passed the ball under Ring Man's wriggling fingers, and Hollywood got it over the line to Topper, who was immediately double-teamed.

I dashed forward faster than I had ever run and managed to get ahead of him by a step. As soon as I crossed the midcourt line, Topper somehow managed to whip the ball over the two men who were hopping and waving around him.

I started to dribble in circles then while the rest of the team spread out to give me clear targets. The crowd, savvy enough to know our strategy, began to boo.

Five seconds went by.

"Don't be chicken," Ring Man growled.

As I went on bouncing the ball, I just smiled. "You want this? Come and get it." His eyes widened angrily and he lunged forward. He came within a whisper of slapping it away, but I managed to whip the ball to Alphonse.

He wasn't really a dribbler, so he tossed it to Topper. When his man came at him, intent on fouling, Topper threw it to the Professor. They played keep-away like that before it wound up back with me.

By then, ten seconds had ticked off.

Ring Man called me every name in the book and some that weren't, but I'd learned my lesson with the Davids and I stayed calm while I kept on dribbling.

"What are you going to show me? Or them?" I asked. "That you're a loser?"

When his eyes widened, I knew my barb had struck home. He and I were even more alike than I'd guessed.

And his eyes grew wider and wider as the anger built inside him, knowing that every few bounces was another second gone.

Fifteen seconds to go now.

"You're so lousy that I didn't have to cheat," I grinned.

Swearing at me, he thrust his hand forward as if it were the tip of a fencing foil, but I managed to pivot away in time.

"Too slow," I said and whispered, "loser." I knew exactly how to get his goat now—because the things I said were things that would have gotten to me before I met Jack.

Ten seconds.

I could almost see the steam coming from his ears when I did my best imitation of Jack's smirk. "Can you count to ten? Because that's how long it's going to be before everyone knows what a loser you are."

With a scream, Ring Man rushed at me, so I tried to pass the ball to Alphonse, but Ring Man had only been faking his charge. He had been waiting for me to do just that and he exploded upward to swat the ball from the air.

In dismay, I watched the ball hop away from me. From the corner of my eye, I saw a blur as he threw himself at it. I flung myself forward, not at the ball but at him. I'd hoped to knock him in a different direction, but I only added force to his leap.

He gave a shout of triumph as he snagged the ball before it bounced out-of-bounds. Only, he couldn't stop his momentum, which carried him over the sideline and into a big pipe that ran up the wall. I heard an ugly crack and then he screamed in agony. When I looked, he lay writhing on the floor with his leg at an unnatural angle.

I stood in a daze while the ref called time and his team came running over. The place had gone dead quiet so that everyone could hear him groaning as he asked, "Did we get the ball?"

Dully I heard the ref blow his whistle to begin again, and I felt him stuff the ball into my arms. "Here."

Ring Man was lying on the floor near the sideline, but I think the agony in his eyes wasn't caused so much by the pain but by the fact that they were going to lose.

I turned my back on him and hunched my shoulders, trying to hide from that look. One of his teammates came over to guard me. "You did that on purpose," he glared.

I wanted to say it was an accident, but the words caught in my throat. All I could do was bounce the ball under his flailing arm to Topper. Then, as he began to dribble out the rest of the clock, I stumbled back onto the court.

I barely registered when the game was over. I was just glad to sit back on the bench. There wasn't any sign of Jack and when I asked where he was, Alphonse shrugged. "He was gone before the game ended."

"Making sure he gets his money, I guess," Hollywood said wearily.

It was ugly trying to leave the auditorium after the game. Topper didn't try to sell his photographs. He took one peek outside and stepped back, looking pretty grim.

"We'd better stay in a group, fellas," he said.

He and the rest of the team waited in the room we were using to get changed, and then we went out together. The white townsfolk had all disappeared, so it was just the other team's fans forming a wall between us and our car. From the ugly expressions on their faces, they intended to take out their heroes' defeat on us.

To his credit, Topper went first. "Flash, Barney, you get behind us," he instructed, and then to the rest of the team, he said, "Flying wedge, guys." He and the others had played club football together, as well, so they took up positions to either side of Topper and slightly behind with Topper at the point and them forming the wings with Barney and me like the precious ballcarriers.

Protected on both sides by my teammates, I really felt it was "us" against the world as we marched in a compact bunch. I could trust them not only on the court but off—as long as I stayed away from poker.

I thought it had been bad back in the Windmills' town, but this was a modern gauntlet like the ones I'd read about in history books. Someone spat and the spittle made it past the living wall to hit me on the shoulder. Someone else swung at me but hit the Professor instead. He stumbled but went on determinedly.

Suddenly we heard Annie squealing her battle cry. *A-rooga-a-rooga!*

The night turned bright as she blinded the crowd with her headlights, momentarily stunning them. As Annie bravely chugged forward, she got as many dents as we did, but she forced the crowd back until she halted beside us. We all piled in through doors or windows.

"Thought we'd need to make a quick getaway," Jack said as he threw her into reverse.

We didn't breathe sighs of relief until we'd chugged

out of the reservation. Somehow in the chaos of board-
ing Annie, I'd wound up next to Jack in the front seat. I
turned, looking at the battered faces around me, glad I
was with them. "Thanks, guys."

"Merry Christmas," Topper said, nursing a fat lip. He
looked at the others and then said, "No more reservations,
Jack. They're way too dangerous. Even if it's against a
white team and we're just using the hall there."

Jack was still in a combative mood after Ring Man.
"Beggars can't be choosers. We play wherever we can."

"Or," Topper warned ominously, "we don't play at all."

Jack had pressed his lips together firmly as if he
were trying to lock all the angry words inside. So did
Topper and the others. I felt the hairs on the back of my
neck stand up like they had when I was in Concepcion
during a rare thunderstorm. Any moment, it seemed
like the tension would transform into a destructive
lightning bolt.

Only it didn't.

One by one, muttering and grumbling to one another,
the others fell asleep, but I couldn't join them because I
couldn't shake the memory of those last few minutes of
the game. Finally, when I heard everyone else snoring, I
asked Jack, "Do you know what happened to that point
guard?"

"I heard they were taking him to a hospital," Jack said.
"He'll probably always have a limp now."

"So his playing days are done too," I said in shock. I thought of all that anger bottled up inside him with no way out. "That's going to kill him. I've never met anyone who wanted to win so bad. I felt so sorry for him when he got hurt."

"Enough to give his team the ball?" Jack asked.

I slumped in the seat. "Of course not."

"I didn't think so." He stared straight ahead at the road. "I lost my head back there, but you did good, kid."

I knew he wasn't referring to my play but to taking out Ring Man. He thought I had hurt Ring Man deliberately. Suddenly I felt filthy with more than just dried sweat.

"For what I did?" I asked in a small voice.

"For doing what I said," he said firmly.

As we drove on, I glanced around me, but the others were still sleeping, exhausted from what had been a battle rather than a game.

"You do much of *that* yourself?" I asked.

"And had it done to me," he admitted. "How do you think I got my bum leg?"

I rubbed my head, wishing I could scrub away all my dark thoughts. "I just keep wondering what I would do without basketball. It's all I'm good at."

He glanced at me. "There's no place for a tender conscience now. The spotlight just burns it away."

I didn't have much use for my conscience and yet I didn't want to lose it—even if it meant I wasn't going to get everything I wanted. I wished real bad that I could talk to Jean rather than Jack, but she was over a thousand miles away.

I closed my eyes so I wouldn't have to listen to him anymore, but I still couldn't sleep. I kept hearing the bone breaking and the guard screaming.

After a couple of hours, we stopped so Topper could take over the wheel from Jack and so the rest of us could stretch. I still had all these dark thoughts tumbling around inside my head. I needed to speak to someone bad, but I couldn't talk to the other Dragons, not even Barney. More than ever, I wished Jean were here.

Since she wasn't, I'd have to write a postcard.

Squatting by the headlights, I tried to put down what was bothering me, but I told you I was lousy with words. All I could manage was: *A lot's happened. Wish we could chat.*

I stared at the skimpy lines, feeling frustrated. I was a basketball player, not a writer.

If Jean had been here, she would have put everything into perspective for me and known exactly what to say to cheer me up. I hadn't realized how much I'd come to depend on her, but Grandpa Joe had once told me about an invisible string that connected a guy and a gal. Suddenly, despite the long miles, I'd never felt closer to her.

I tried to think of how to tell her that, but I'm no good with mush, so I wound up writing, *Miss you.*

It seemed so inadequate to express what I was feeling. Desperately, I underlined *Miss* several times because I really meant it this time.

And then Topper was honking the horn and shouting from behind the wheel, "Flash, let's go!"

I'd been signing my cards with *Your Pal* or *Your Chum* but that didn't seem enough so I dashed off, *Guess Who?*, and then pocketed the card and squeezed back in among my snoring teammates.

Okay, okay, I know it was dopey, but I told you I was lousy with words.

CHAPTER | XIII

The next morning I had second thoughts about that postcard, but when I tried to tear it up, I couldn't find it.

We were in the washroom of a gas station taking turns to clean up. Barney saw me searching through my bag.

"If you're looking for your agent's fee, I found it in the car, so I just put it in the mailbox outside," Barney said.

I looked at him, both angry and afraid. "Did you read it?"

He splashed water on his face from the basin. "Why would I? It's all the same stuff anyway."

"Uh, yeah," I said lamely. "That's right."

"I still think you owe her more," Barney grumbled as he repacked his bag. "After all, she is taking care of your dad."

"That's none of your business," I snapped.

Now that the postcard had been sent, though, it didn't seem right to go back to my prewritten stuff so, when Barney wasn't looking, I chucked the postcards into the garbage can. Then I popped into the gas station and bought some more.

I actually felt kind of relieved that I was going to have to write new postcards, because there were so many thoughts and feelings whirling around inside my head. Maybe I could squeeze some of them onto the cards to Jean so when we got back we could talk. She was the only one who wouldn't make fun of me.

Jack wired his partner, the accountant, for money, but he didn't get any replies. Meals got skimpier and rarer, and then it was usually a pound of baloney and a loaf of bread that we bought collectively. Jack even saved on our gas by coasting in neutral on any down slope.

We were all hoping for a big payoff on New Year's Eve, but the few people who ventured out in that town wanted to celebrate another year of surviving the Depression. We had maybe twenty people scattered in the stands so we knew Jack would miss yet another payroll.

As we left for the next town, we could hear the whooping from the Masons Hall, where they were holding a dance. It didn't help the team's mood that we didn't have enough money for a bottle of soda pop.

The next couple of weeks made us feel more and

more jinxed because we each started to get injured. The Professor was hobbled after twisting his ankle. I'd hurt my left wrist when I'd fallen in a game. Topper had banged up his right shoulder. It was never anything to end a Dragon's tour, but it put him out for a game or two. And we always had five members so we didn't have to forfeit a game, but that meant those five had to play the entire game and watch out for fouls.

Maybe it was the combination of the cold, the frustration, the hunger, the travel, and the exhaustion, or maybe it was just because they were fed up with not getting paid for a month, but the rest of the Dragons hardly spoke to Jack, except during a game. Instead, they complained to one another in loud tones so Jack could overhear them.

Because the Dragons thought of me as his pet, they gave me the same cold shoulder. The only one I could "talk" to was Jean, so I really worked hard on my postcards, but I never did know what to say. I just hoped she could see that I was trying.

Then came that fateful afternoon when we blew a tire in the middle of nowhere. It was the match that set off the bomb's fuse.

"There," Jack said when Alphonse and Barney had finished changing it. "The wheel's as good as new."

Topper squatted down, inspecting the spare. "The patches have got patches." He fingered a spot. "And the inner tube's showing through here."

"It'll do," Jack said in a level voice. He always took that tone as a signal to end the discussion. Only this time, Topper wouldn't let go.

"No," he said. "We don't go anywhere and we don't play games until you replace the tires."

"But don't you understand? There's no money." Jack ran a frustrated hand through his thinning hair. "All we got is Annie and whatever gas is in the tank."

"Even if we believed you, it's not safe," Topper argued.

"We can fix the tires once the weather warms up and the crowds start coming again," Jack pleaded.

"Warm weather won't do us any good if we get killed before that," Topper snapped. "No, we're tired of your empty promises. Either start keeping your word or we're finished playing for you."

Jack turned desperately to the rest of us. "I guess Topper's quitting the team. We'll have to play with just five guys."

The Dragons glanced at one another nervously before the Professor finally cleared his throat. "We're with Tops."

"So put up or shut up," Topper growled to Jack.

Barney nodded his head with the others, so he was sticking with them as well.

Jack sucked in his breath like he'd been hit right in the breadbasket. Then he let it out slow. He was one guy who knew how to roll with the punches. "Then I'll find some mugs who want to play." He jerked his head at me. "Come on, Flash. We'll get replacements in the next town. I'll even suit up myself, gimpy leg and all. I can always make up some story about why the rest of the team isn't Chinese. We'll play the style I want."

"Please, Jack, you can't just dump them," I appealed.

"They're the ones dumping us," Jack argued.

I looked at Barney, but he just folded his arms like he was staying put. He was more than my partner. He was my brother. I couldn't leave him to freeze.

"You're losing your temper again, Jack," I said, trying to calm him down. "We can work it out if we just talk some more."

He slapped his leg in exasperation. "I don't need them, just a name that'll draw the crowds."

"If he doesn't need us, he doesn't need you," Alphonse warned me.

Jack dismissed him with a wave of his hand. "Didn't I take care of you, kid?" he asked me.

"You got something out of it too," I said.

Jack scratched the tip of his nose. "What's this really about? That Indian kid still bothering you? I told you: I shouldn't have gotten angry. I'm sorry. Okay?"

"But what happens next time when a big game's on the line?" I wondered. "Would you give me the same orders?"

Jack hesitated. "Winning's what counts. You do what you have to."

I didn't like the road he was showing me. His spotlight shone bright on one spot, but the rest of it was shadows. And the further I went, the darker it would get.

"Let's stay and work it out with everybody," I urged.

"You're not taking their side?" he asked in disbelief. "After all I've done for you."

I remembered, though, what he had threatened during that game with the Native Americans, and I knew I couldn't trust him—but I could trust the other Dragons. "And what happens if I don't obey you now? Are you going to replace me too?"

"Don't talk loony. I treated you like you were my own son," he insisted.

It was the wrong thing to say. I didn't want to be his or anyone's kid. Maybe I had been leaning too much on Jack. It was time for me to be my own man again, especially when Jack was doing something wrong. "You can't boss me around anymore."

He looked hurt so he lashed back. "You want to stay a snot-nosed punk all your life?"

He had nerve. "And become what, Jack? You?" I waved a hand at his leg and then at Annie and then at the wasteland around us. "An old bum in the middle of nowhere?"

"So you're just another dumb loser after all," Jack smirked, as if this was the greatest joke of all.

"You're the one who bet on me," I shot back at him. "So what does that make you?"

"The biggest, dumbest loser of all." His smirk widened into a sad smile. "The laugh's really on me, isn't it?"

We watched, stunned, as he jerked open the trunk and began to throw our gear onto the snow by the roadside. The Professor gathered up his precious bag of books. "Are you crazy?"

Jack slammed the trunk down. "Naw, I've finally come to my senses. I'm gonna sell this heap and get a train ticket. I just hope I can get enough to make it home."

"But what about us?" I asked.

Jack got into the car. "You're on your own now, boys. The Dragons, the tour, the bills, and the head-aches are all yours."

Alphonse jumped on the running board. "How'll we get there if you take the car?"

"Shank's mare," Jack said, and tried to start the engine. Except Annie gave a dry rattle. That didn't stop Jack, who kept trying and trying until he flooded the engine. Frustrated, he jumped out and kicked the fender, swearing at the car, the team, and the Almighty—not necessarily in that order.

Then he flung open the trunk again, yanked out his bag, and began limping down the highway, turning around every now and then and stumbling backward with his thumb up in the air.

We watched him silently until he passed out of sight. I felt this lump inside my throat like I'd swallowed a boulder.

Barney seemed close to tears. "It can't be over."

I was ready to cry myself. The spotlight was gone and I was just plain Calvin Chin again, the good-for-nothing son of a drunk who didn't have anything the world wanted— not his book smarts, not his ability to bounce a basketball.

And then it really hit me. We were in the middle of nowhere. Chinatown might as well have been as far away as the moon. "It's done, Barney."

"Did you deliberately hurt that other kid?" Barney asked me.

"It was an accident," I insisted, but I could see the others weren't sure about that. "You're not calling me a liar, are you?"

Barney took longer then I would have liked before he said, "I guess I got to believe my partner."

Alphonse tried to act the peacemaker. "Now's no time to fight among ourselves."

Hollywood turned and pulled open the car hood. "Maybe I can fix Annie long enough to get us to the nearest town."

Topper joined him. "Then we can sell her and get some tickets home."

"Or as close as we can get," Alphonse said.

It was nearly sunset before Hollywood had Annie chugging away for our last ride. As we rattled down the road, we kept an eye out for Jack, but he was long gone. "He must've gotten a lift," the Professor said.

"No car passed by us, though," Hollywood said.

"Then the wolves got him," Topper grunted as he drove. He didn't sound upset.

"Not a chance. I bet you no self-respecting wolf would want a taste of Jack," Barney laughed.

"It'd be a sucker bet," Topper agreed as he nursed Annie along.

The scrub brush and wasteland rolled by forever, deepening in color as the sun set until the sky was a blaze of oranges and reds.

"You'd never see a sunset like this in Chinatown," the Professor said wistfully. "I'm going to miss this. And the night sky too. The city lights drown out the stars."

"Back to washing dishes and carrying the slop out of the restaurant," Hollywood sighed.

"At least you got a job in your uncle's joint," Alphonse said.

"That's the way it goes," Topper said over his shoulder. "One day you're Hawaiian royalty touring the world, and the next you're sleeping in doorways and pounding the pavement looking for a job and your next meal."

There was a gloomy silence as we all thought about our lack of prospects. "I guess it's back to hustling suckers," Barney said to me.

I was already having second thoughts about turning my back on Jack. The one time I tried to do the right thing, I'd dumped my future into a garbage can. I'd

always been so smart and played the odds. Why did I
have to be a noble idiot all of a sudden? As Hardy liked to
say to Laurel, this was another fine mess I'd gotten into. I
liked being Flash and now I was just plain Calvin again.

"I'm tired of that, of basketball, of everything," I said.

When Barney scratched his head, his elbow brushed
my ear. "How you going to eat?"

"I don't know." I shrugged. "Maybe I'll take a long
walk off a short pier."

At that moment, Annie finally gave up with a last
cough and rattle, rolling to a halt. As the sky grew a deep
purple, Hollywood began emergency surgery by the faint
light of the moon and the stars—squinting and sometimes
even working by feel alone in the growing darkness.

"Shooting star," the Professor said, pointing over our
heads.

"Time to make your wishes, boys," Topper said.

I glared at him. Even now, he was still trying to boss
me around like he was the coach—only there wasn't a
team anymore. I was sick of him, of them, even of Barney.
Most of all, I was sick of myself.

"I'm done wishing too," I said. I got my bag out of
the trunk.

"Where you going?" Barney asked anxiously.

I pointed to the horizon, where lights glowed faintly.
"There must be a town nearby, unless the wolves have figured out how to make campfires."

"Hollywood'll get the car running, kid," Alphonse said, "so hold your horses."

"I don't do anything with others anymore," I said sourly. "From now on, my team is me."

"What about your share of Annie?" Hollywood asked.

Suddenly I was as sick of them as I was of Jack. I needed to be alone. "You'd be lucky to get two dimes for this heap. I'm not waiting around for any more empty promises." I jerked my head at Barney. "You coming?"

Barney glanced from me to the others. "I . . . I think I'll wait."

Well, I'd just said I wasn't into doing stuff with anyone ever again. I guess that included Barney too. But somehow hearing him say that hurt even more. "Suit yourself. Just do yourself a favor and keep away from the card games." I slammed the trunk shut.

I lost sight of them real quick. Even the asphalt road faded into the dim light, so I felt like I was walking where no human had ever walked before. Somewhere a wolf howled, and I thought of Grandpa Joe's stories about Wyoming when he'd mined coal here. The packs picked off Chinese who wandered too far away from camps.

I pulled up my collar because it had grown real cold with the sun down. I'd joined the team partly to escape Chinatown and all those nagging Guests. Well, I'd gotten my wish. I was all by myself in the middle of nowhere.

I missed Jean and Grandpa Joe. Even my old man. So maybe I needed Chinatown and home after all. It was like a bum knee. It might bother you, but you still needed it to stand.

I wrapped my arms around myself, putting my hands into my armpits for warmth. My feet grew numb until I couldn't even feel them anymore. So I took one step at a time. Just keep moving forward, I urged myself.

As I plodded on, I recalled Jack's poetical flight of fancy so long ago. The Dragon Road sure was hard. And especially when you were alone. I hoped he was okay, wherever he was. He'd tried to look out for me, even if it had been in his own self-interest. I hoped he'd understand one day that I just couldn't do things his way. But knowing Jack, hell would have to freeze over before he forgave me.

I felt a twinge when I remembered my promise to Grandpa Joe that I would watch out for Barney. It seemed like I was failing at everything.

I can't say how long I hoofed it, but it felt like forever and the town's lights didn't seem to grow any closer. Overhead the sky deepened from violet to black and the stars shone so bright and clear that they seemed etched on my eyeballs. I managed to pick out the Big Dipper. I didn't know a lot about the Chinese legends except what Grandpa Joe had told me. Back in China they called it the Rice Measure Basket. Basketball had gotten its name because Dr. Naismith, the inventor of the game, had used peach baskets. So I guess the Measuring Basket was a cager's constellation in a way, and at first I took it for a good sign. Then I realized I was getting light-headed from the cold and exhaustion, and I gave my head a shake to clear out the cobwebs.

Still, when you're all alone like that and feeling like the last human on earth, you have to think. Okay, so maybe I was a miserable excuse for a human being, but if I survived the night, I'd try to do better.

I guess it was some trick of the light or the horizon, but as I finally headed up over a swell of land, the town suddenly stood before me. It wasn't exactly San Francisco, but lights blazed in windows and street lamps glowed.

It was another one of those sleepy towns where they rolled the sidewalk up at night, but there couldn't have been much to it even in the daylight. There was a shop to buy groceries, a gas station, a drugstore with a soda fountain, a tiny movie theater calling itself the Melodeum. The biggest place in town was the hardware and feed store. My stomach gave a growl as I passed by a greasy-spoon diner. But everything was buttoned up tight, and even if they'd been open, I didn't have any dough to get something to eat—not even a dime to use for a telephone call.

Then, as I stood on the street corner under the streetlight, I heard a familiar sound. I figured the homesickness was making me hallucinate, but I could hear it—the faint *clack-clack* of mah jong tiles hitting one another as they were mixed up for a new game.

I followed the sound down a dim street, breaking into a trot in my eagerness, not caring if I tripped in the darkness. Then I felt gravel under my feet and I saw a red light in the distance by a railroad tower. Boxcars loomed around me like wooden mastodons, but I kept stumbling on until I came to a cluster of a half-dozen buildings. A couple of them were boarded up, but I could have cried when I saw the others.

In the light pouring from the windows, I saw Chinese words underneath the English ones on the signs. One of the buildings was a flophouse like the two boarded-up ones, but the fourth was a small chop suey joint and the fifth was a general store.

The game, though, seemed to be in the laundry, where an old man was teasing someone in Chinese. It was a tiny Chinatown—the kind that Grandpa Joe had said used to cover the Western states until the Americans had destroyed them. Somehow this one had survived.

However, I lost my nerve when I got to the door of the laundry. I looked so grubby—and I smelled grubby too. How could I go in? I was just a beggar.

But at that moment, the door jerked open, tinkling a little bell inside, and an elderly man stood there with a long Chinese pipe in his hand. *"Ah Sam,"* he said in Chinese to someone behind him, *"you've got a customer. And from the looks of his clothes, he really needs you."*

Another, even more ancient man shuffled forward, in a pair of worn open-heeled Chinese slippers. Dragons had been embroidered on the tops at one time; but most of them had worn away so it was only an outline.

"What do you want, boy?" he asked. *"You do speak Chinese, don't you?"*

I just stood there, tongue-tied. The moist, warm, soapy air reminded me of the laundries in Chinatown. It made me feel homesick and nervous at the same time. I felt my shoulders tensing waiting for yet another scolding from a Guest.

"Either bring him in or shut the door," a third man called. *"You're letting out the heat."*

Ah Sam motioned me inside. *"You better come in, boy. If Ah Bing catches a cold, we'll have to take care of him."*

Pipe Man shook his head. *"And he'll whine all the time."*

Despite the heat in the laundry, Ah Bing sat bundled up in a muffler and coat as if he were sitting on a snow bank instead of on a stool. *"At our age, we have to be careful of pneumonia,"* he said defensively.

A teapot was keeping warm on a small stove. *"You want something to drink?"* the Pipe Man asked kindly.

"This isn't your laundry anymore, Ah Chen," Ah Sam snapped at him. *"It's mine. I'll offer the tea to him."*

"It won't be your laundry much longer if you lose the next hand," Ah Chen countered.

Ah Bing motioned for me to sit on a stool. *"You cuckoos are both renting castles in the clouds. I'm the one who's going to beat you both."*

"I say we ought to both work together to make sure he doesn't win," Ah Chen grumbled to Ah Sam. *"He always puts too much starch into the clothes. And then the customers complain about the chafing."*

Muffler Man defended himself. *"Better starch in a collar than in cashew chicken."*

Ah Sam shuffled over to the stove. *"Can I help if it the laundry starch box looks like the cornstarch?"*

"You need glasses, that's what you need," Ah Chen said and sat down to help the Muffler Man begin to stack up the mah jong tiles into the "walls" of a square.

Ah Sam poured out a cup of tea and brought it over. I drank it thirstily and with relish. It wasn't any of that rotgut orange pekoe I'd put up with in so many towns. This was real oolong.

"Thanks," I croaked, wiping my mouth with the back of my hand.

Suddenly Ah Sam thrust his face close to mine and squinted. *"You're you."*

"Are you going to play?" Ah Chen demanded, rubbing his hands together. *"I can't wait to take the deed away from you."*

However, Ah Sam walked over to the counter, the slippers slapping against his heels. *"It's him,"* he said, jabbing a finger at me.

"Him who?" Ah Bing asked, staring at me.

"Him!" Ah Sam hunted through a stack of bills and receipts stuck through a long spike until he found what he was looking for. He held out one of the Dragons fliers. *"He plays ball with a basket."*

"It's basketball, you ignorant turnip," Ah Chen corrected him and swung around on his stool to gaze at me. *"What's a famous man like you doing here at this time of night?"*

"Why else? He's come here to eat." Ah Sam grabbed the end of Ah Bing's scarf and tickled his face with it. *"Go cook him something."*

Ah Bing sneezed as he pulled back. *"Why me? I run the store."*

"You lost that last week, fool," Ah Chen said. *"You're handling the restaurant now."*

Ah Bing scratched under his wool cap. *"Did I? I lose track sometimes."*

"I could use a snack too," Ah Sam said. *"Make a lot."*

"I . . . I haven't got any dough," I confessed and got ready for them to throw me out.

They looked a little puzzled that a celebrity wouldn't have money, but Ah Chen said, *"You don't have to pay. It's us who ought to thank you. You can catch us up to date on the latest slang. Ours is twenty years old."*

Ah Sam chimed in. *"And the gossip! Tell us what's been happening in Chinatown. And then about where you've been and what you've seen,"* Ah Sam said. *"It's always these two's sour faces all the time."*

"Don't tell them until I'm done cooking," Ah Bing warned, *"or I'll spit into the wok."*

We moved next door to the restaurant, where the chairs and tables looked even older than the three men. While Ah Bing chopped and clanked happily in the kitchen, the other two got around to the standard quiz every Chinese will throw at another: Who was my family and where did they come from? So I gave them a heavily edited version that passed inspection.

Then Ah Chen pointed at Barney's picture on the flier. *"I've been meaning to ask you. This Barney Young, is he any relation to Joseph?"*

"He's his grandson," I said innocently. *"Do you know Grandpa—I mean, Mr. Joseph Young?"*

From their astonished faces, it was like I'd said I was the buddy of the lost Ming emperor of China.

"My father worked with his father, Otter, on the railroad, you know," Ah Bing boasted.

"And our fathers worked with his uncle Foxfire in the California goldfields," Ah Chen said, nodding to Ah Sam.

I scratched my head, embarrassed. Grandpa Joe had told us about his family who had been in America since the Gold Rush, but I'd always slept through history in school—not that there was anything in our textbooks— and I hadn't done much better when Grandpa Joe tried to reminisce. *"Yeah, I think I heard something about that."*

"When you see him," Ah Chen requested, *"you tell him that we always read him even if we don't always agree with him."*

"And the Chinese newspapers might be a month old when they get to us," Ah Sam added.

Back in San Francisco, Barney and I would stumble in sometimes at two in the morning, and there would be Grandpa Joe writing at a kitchen table. We figured he was just caught up in another one of his crackpot causes. I had no idea that Grandpa Joe was publishing articles and columns for newspapers around America in either Chinese or English. Wherever there was an injustice, you could count on him to speak up.

I'd seen for myself that Grandpa Joe had contacts around the country through the Y. But I never thought about the Chinese, because in San Francisco a lot of people thought Grandpa Joe was a little crazy. However, these old geezers in the middle of nowhere counted on Grandpa Joe to keep them connected to what was happening to other Chinese. I wondered just how many other Guests in little Chinatowns across the country depended on him for the same thing. It was just like Uncle Quail's tide pools on his reef. Each was a separate little world and yet they were linked by a trickle of water, running from one pool to the other, and among isolated Guests like them, the link was Grandpa Joe.

I wish Grandpa Joe had been there to hear what he meant to them. They were why he wrote into the late hours, even though he must have been tired. Too bad he didn't have more readers like these three Guests. But then

I knew what he'd say: that it didn't matter how many people read him, only that someone did.

Well, any buddy of Grandpa Joe's was a buddy of theirs. Ah Bing cooked up a storm and then heaped the table with bowls of chicken, shrimp, barbecued pork, mushrooms, bamboo shoots, and vegetables. I'd never had much use for vegetables before, but now I found I craved Chinese greens, especially bok choy.

It was family-style with everyone reaching in with their chopsticks. For old guys, their fingers moved pretty nimbly—especially when it came to a choice bit of meat. What they lacked in quickness, they made up for in wiles, so I knew I was going to have my work cut out for me.

When someone won a particularly nice tidbit, they teased the others, including me—it hadn't taken long for my celebrity to wear off. Between mouthfuls, I kept my end of the bargain by telling them the latest Chinatown gossip and slang. They especially relished the swear words for their mah jong games.

By that point, I was feeling comfortable enough to ask them the question that had been bothering me. *"So why are you here?"*

They told me that the Chinese had settled here long ago when they had helped build the railroad through here, and it had prospered for a number of years—not only for Chinese railroad workers but for miners and farmhands. But then the Americans had turned on the Chinese all over the West, and even though this Chinatown had been burned to the ground, the American who owned the land had the courage to defy his neighbors and let the Chinese rebuild again.

"Didn't you want to leave?" I asked.

"It's our home too," Ah Sam said. *"Our families were here long before most of the Americans came."*

And somehow when most of the jobs for Chinese had dried up, the Chinatown had survived because their customers were those same American neighbors.

When they could have gone home, they didn't have the money; and when they had enough cash, revolutions and wars had sealed off China, so the three men were trapped.

"How are your families doing back there?" I asked.

There was a moment of silence and both men looked sad. *"We don't know. We haven't heard from them in a year."* They didn't have to go on. The Japanese controlled that area now.

Me and my big mouth. Hurriedly, I changed the subject. *"So what's this about swapping businesses?"*

To escape the boredom, the three Guests gambled, winning and losing the laundry, store, and restaurant so many times that they had forgotten who had owned what originally. When someone lost his place, he ran one of the others, so that by now all three were capable of running any of the three establishments.

I wanted to thank them for all they had done for me, but I didn't have Grandpa Joe's gift for gab—and I didn't have much practice at it anyway. All I could do was stammer, *"Th-thank you."* I hadn't expected to find such kindness in the middle of nowhere and certainly not from Guests. I fumbled for something more to say . . . when I heard a familiar mechanical coughing.

I shot up from my chair, knocking it over so it banged on the floor.

Noodles dangled from Ah Chen's mouth when he spoke. *"What's the matter? The food's not that bad."*

I was already striding to the door, and I threw it open eagerly—just in time to see Annie chugging around the corner, her headlights beaming like tiny but powerful moons.

I ran across the wooden sidewalk and jumped into the street to wave my arms. Topper tooted the horn in answer, and then I remembered how bad the brakes were and hopped back onto the sidewalk as Annie struggled to a stop.

"How'd you find this place?" I asked.

Alphonse stuck his head out a window with a laugh. "We followed Barney's nose."

Barney tapped the side of his nose. "This nose knows."

Ah Chen turned to Ah Bing, *"Better—"*

Ah Bing frowned. *"I know, I know, I'll cook some more food. Don't tell me what to do in my own restaurant."*

"It's yours until we finish the last game," Ah Sam laughed.

I jumped onto Annie's running board and grabbed Barney by the arm so that his head poked out the window. *"And this is Joseph Young's grandson."*

The three Guests had been nice to me, but they acted like Barney was royalty. Even at our best moments, Topper and I hadn't been treated so well. They stuffed him and everybody else and made me eat another meal too until we couldn't move from our chairs.

"So," Ah Bing said, *"now you're back together again. You can sleep here tonight if you like and still be where you need to be for the game tomorrow."* Like any Guests, they figured they could boss younger Chinese around.

Topper scratched his cheek. *"I don't think we can make it that far. Our car's held together with wire, bubble gum, and rags. We barely got here."*

Ah Chen was rising from the table. *"I'll get Frank Renaldo. Ah Sam, show them the way to his garage."*

Topper gave a cough. *"We . . . we can't pay him, though."*

Shamefaced, I explained, *"The audiences haven't been so good lately."*

Ah Sam had also gotten up. *"We'll take care of Frank."*

"We'll repay you somehow," Topper promised.

Ah Sam straightened indignantly. *"We didn't ask for payment."*

Ah Bing turned to Barney. *"Does your grandfather write to make money?"*

Barney squirmed. *"No, he doesn't get a cent."*

Ah Bing nodded. *"If you do something, you shouldn't do it for wealth or fame. You do it because it's the right thing to do. And that's why we're helping you."*

"And perhaps you don't get the big crowds you should," Ah Chen said encouragingly. *"But you must get some people. And those are the ones who really want to see you."*

"The ones who want our autographs," I said softly.

"Your autographs?" Ah Chen mused and turned to his friends. *"Isn't that something? People are learning that Chinese can be more than cooks or laundrymen or storekeepers."*

Okay, so maybe there was a time not too long ago when I would have thought he belonged on the junk pile because he was too old, but he and his friends had saved our lives. I let his words sink in. Basketball wasn't as big as Grandpa Joe's writing, but it was all I had.

Maybe I was acting like a chump, but lately I'd been playing it smart and hadn't liked myself much. Maybe it was time to try it the other way. "I say we play the game," I said, looking around, "even if we have to hitchhike."

One by one the others nodded their heads.

"We'll probably have to use our thumbs anyway," the Professor sighed. "Why would Frank open up in the middle of the night?"

"Frank's a good mechanic, but a terrible poker player," Ah Chen said, and winked. *"Guess who owes us money? We don't play mah jong all the time, you know."*

PART THREE

The Dragons

CHAPTER | XIV

The promoter almost hopped for joy when we rolled into town. "Where've you been? I've been calling all over the state trying to find you." He looked around. "Hey, where's Jack?"

"He quit," Topper said. "The contract's with us now."

The promoter got a worried look. "But somebody's got to be in charge."

"I guess this big lug is," I said, jerking a thumb at Topper, and the others nodded.

We didn't have any money for lunch and wouldn't have even gotten there if Ah Bing hadn't talked Frank into throwing in a free tank of gas.

Fortunately, the three old-timers had packed a huge meal for us, so we didn't have to play on empty bellies. Sure enough, the three Guests showed up with Frank, who had driven them down and was explaining basket-ball to them. When I waved, I saw there were another dozen people clustered around them high up in a corner of the bleachers, who were also helping Frank with the explanations. I guess the Guests had talked them into coming too.

The promoter bustled over about then and held out a slip of paper. "Better sign this."

I figured he wanted it for his kid. "Sure, who do you want it to?"

"It's not an autograph, it's a bill," the promoter said and jerked his head up toward the bleachers. "They said you were treating all of them."

I turned with a groan. "They probably don't even know what basketball is." Ah Chen waved to me and then nudged the others, who also began to wave to their benefactor.

"And there's more coming in." Topper winced as another half dozen came through the door, and the old-timers beckoned them up to their rooting section.

We owed them for saving our lives but, even so, we could wind up owing money for tonight. "I hope they didn't invite the whole town."

I really wanted to put on a show, but we ran like our feet were in buckets of cement and we dropped passes like our hands had turned to wood. The other team was a bunch of stiffs, but by the end of the quarter they were up on us by five points.

The Professor got the tip-off and tossed the ball to me, and for once that night I managed to hold on to it. Then, suddenly, from up in the bleachers, I heard the three old-timers calling out, "Up the Chinese!" And then Frank and their friends took it up too, mangling the pronunciation, but they were enthusiastic and were having such fun that some of the home crowd even started trying to chant it and were stamping their feet.

When I ran down the court, I felt like there was a wind blowing me along. I realized that my old man had been wrong. Even if you're born alone, you don't have to die alone.

From their grins, the other Dragons were feeling just as good, and pretty soon the score was even. I was finding that I could read them now as easily as I did Barney. On a break, I knew where they were going to be and how they liked the ball passed to them. By halftime, we were up by three, and eight by the end of the game.

Ah Bing pounded me on the back, but I couldn't understand him through his scarf. His partners were both hoarse from shouting, but Ah Chen managed to croak, "I couldn't have been prouder if you were my own son."

"You mean grandson, you old fossil," Ah Sam teased.

I'm not a sloppy kind of guy who likes talking about what he's feeling, but I was just so grateful for what they had said. "And I couldn't have been prouder than if you were my grandpops," I said—and meant it.

Later, the promoter was all smiles as he came into the locker room to pay us. "You boys can play in this town any time you like." He jerked his thumb toward the street. "And the postmaster's waiting outside. He said there's a package for a couple of you."

Topper paused in unbuttoning his shirt. "Did he remember the names?"

He scratched his head. "If he told me, I forget. Had a lot on my mind, you know. But he said you could pick it up tomorrow morning."

"That's a problem," Topper said. "We got to leave tonight if we're going to make the next town." Jack had set up the tour, and his notes were still in the car, so it would just be a question of following them.

"So drive a little faster," the Professor said, and the others nodded. The mention of a package had made us a little homesick.

"Yeah, I guess I could." Topper was suddenly as eager as the rest of the team to get that little bit of home. "Flash, you get the package and hustle back as quick as you can. Alphonse, you give Barney a hand loading up the car."

"Why don't I get the package?" Alphonse complained.

"Because Flash runs faster than you, Flat Foot. He can be there and back before you even get halfway," Topper snapped.

The promoter took me outside, where a tall man was waiting with two excited kids. "This is Mack, the postmaster."

"My kids were hoping to talk to you." He stuck out a paw that was twice as big as mine. "You guys put on quite a show. Yes, sir."

"We aim to please," I grinned.

When the promoter told Mack about our problem, the postmaster shuffled his feet. "Well, it's not quite kosher, but I think I can make an exception in your case. If you want to come to the post office, I'll get it for you."

It felt cold outside after the steamy warmth of the gym. "It's a quiet place," Mack murmured, "but you don't get night skies like this in the city."

"Isn't that the Big Dipper, Daddy?" his daughter asked.

"Yup," Mack said, and pointed out the stars as he and his daughter walked along.

His boy, though, stuck close to me like a silent shadow. I was never good at small talk, but I thought I ought to try. "So you like basketball."

He nodded eagerly but didn't say a word, and he answered all my other questions with nods or shakes or gestures. I was beginning to think the poor kid couldn't talk until his hand suddenly shot up and he said, "Shooting star."

His dad and sister stopped dead in their tracks. "Make a wish."

Their lips moved quietly as the star traced a ribbon of light across the sky as if a seam was splitting open on a black coat. But I was looking at them—the daughter with her hand in her father's and the son standing next to me, each of them so happy, so peaceful because their father would sacrifice his own life to protect them, and his children knew it.

Sometime way back when I was small, I must have been as trusting as these kids, only to have my old man disappoint and hurt me. So I'd grown up never wanting a family because I figured I'd be as rotten a father as my old man. After all, there were times when I could barely stand myself. I thought I'd only wind up warping my kids as much as he warped me.

But seeing the postmaster and his children—well, it made me want to try—so if I ever did have a family, I was going to try to be as good a father as the postmaster. I'd teach my kid everything I knew—which, when you came down to it, was basketball.

And then I was lifting my head as the streak of light began to fade, and I hoped I'd made my wish in time—though it was actually more of a hope.

The post office was a small, brick building, and I waited outside with the children. The boy was just as quiet as before, but his sister chatted away, wanting to know about all the places I had seen. She was like a sponge, soaking up everything. If ever there was a born traveler, it was her.

"That's enough, Ellie," Mack said when he stepped outside again. He had a parcel wrapped in brown paper and red string. "The man's got places to go."

"I know," she sighed. "I wish I were going too."

I didn't tell her about the bone-rattling, tiring journeys. She could learn about that on her own. Right now, she should have the fun of dreaming.

"Ellie collects the stamps of the world," Mack laughed. "One day she's going to see all those countries for herself."

"You bet," she said confidently.

They were heading home from there, so I said goodbye. "Thanks for the special delivery," I said, and shook Mack's hand again and then I took each of the kids' hands in turn.

But as I headed off, the boy suddenly blurted out, "Can I have your autograph?"

Mack rubbed his son's hair affectionately. "He's usually such a chatterbox, but he's too much in awe of you. He's been working up the nerve to ask you the whole night."

"Glad he got it out before he exploded," Ellie added.

I signed a flier for him and then one for Ellie.

As I headed back to the gym, I didn't feel the cold at all and my legs weren't tired. Instead, I felt like I was walking on springs.

I guess it was just as well that I had been the errand boy, because the package was addressed to me and Barney care of the local postmaster. I recognized Jean's neat handwriting. As our agent, she had the list of our tour, so she must have sent it on.

I resisted the urge to rip it open, but Barney couldn't. By then, the team was standing around the car waiting for me. The Professor thoughtfully picked up the scraps and the string and deposited them into a nearby garbage can.

Inside were two notes and a bag of fat cookies an inch thick and about the size of silver dollars. "Food!" someone shouted and immediately four hands shot in.

Poor Barney struggled to hold the box upright as he tried to get one for himself. "Hey, keep your mitts off. Those are Cal's and mine."

"All for one, and one for all," Topper laughed, spraying crumbs all over himself.

Alphonse bit into one and then looked at them, puzzled. "Hey, these are the cookies they make at the Moon Festival." That was sometime in autumn but it was already winter.

"My grandfather's got a baker friend who'd make these out of season if he asked," Barney said as he finally got to gobble one down. I rescued the envelope from the box before someone ate that too. Pasted to the envelope was a cutout of a paper dragon. Grandpa Joe used to make wonderful animals for Barney and me with just a sheet of paper and a pair of scissors. He was a regular artist that way.

They were cheap, little cookies but they made me suddenly think of crisp nights walking through Chinatown with Jean. As I ate the doughy cookie, I opened the note:

Here's a Valentine's Day present from all of us. Tell Jack to

call Grandpa Joe. We've been getting letters from Grandpa

Joe saying that he's refused to pay them. What's wrong?

We're worried.

In the meantime, we sent these cookies because they won't

spoil no matter how long they sit in the post office. Don't say

we don't take care of our clients. Tiger's been reading and

rereading Barney's postcards. I can't say the same about your

early postcards. You've seen one of them, you've seen them all.

I felt a little guilty about how I had cheated her. Funny thing about that was I felt like I'd actually cheated myself. But then I read the postscript.

P.S. I read and reread your last postcard. I miss you too.

The *miss* was underlined several times just like mine had been.

I folded the note up and stowed it carefully in my pocket. I wished I could see her face. At any rate, the first chance I got, I'd tell her what had happened and that Grandpa Joe could call off his holy bill collectors.

When we had polished off the cookies, Topper dusted the last crumbs off his palms. "Time to hit the road again, boys." He nodded to me. "No time for you to clean up, rosebud, so we'll have to put up with you."

"Put him by a window then," Alphonse said, fanning the air with his hand.

I'd like to say the team was all lovey-dovey after that, but the weather stayed lousy, the roads bad, and the crowds small. We basically played for food and gas money, and sometimes we didn't even have enough of that. A couple of times we ran out of gas and had to push Annie to the places we were supposed to play. But it didn't matter. We were all together on our road, the Dragon Road.

After all the newspaper clippings and ballyhoo, it had been hard to write Jean the truth, but I bit the bullet and told her what was happening. After that, there were packages from her waiting for us at the post office when we pulled into some towns. Some days, her packages were the only meals we had.

The accompanying notes from Jean were always concerned and understanding, and if anyone tried to razz me about them, all I had to do was threaten to cut off his share of our supplies and that always shut him up.

It didn't help either that our brutal schedule kept us confined inside a small car for long periods of time. What with one thing or another, we were bound to get on one another's nerves—especially after a loss. Fortunately there weren't many of those. We still had as many blowups in the team as we had blowouts in the tires. Sometimes punches were even thrown, but deep down, we knew we had to depend on one another, so we never let it go beyond a certain point.

We also finally got our revenge on Alphonse for all his pranks. After a game, while he was still showering, we took his clothes, got into Annie, and chugged off. For half a mile, we let him run after us, naked except for his towel.

Finally Barney glanced through the rear window and then said to Topper, who was driving, "Shouldn't we let him in now?"

Topper checked the rearview mirror. "Naw. He's not even puffing. He should be good for another half mile."

Barney looked behind us again. "Oops. He just lost the towel."

Topper grinned. "Then let's make it two miles." And he gunned the motor.

The Professor even came around to our point of view that there wasn't going to be any war in Europe because the British, French, and Germans were still twiddling their thumbs. The reporters were calling it the Phony War or even the Sitzkrieg—as opposed to the Blitzkrieg when the German tanks had swarmed all over poor Poland.

Current events meant less to us than the humble monuments built by the Chinese years before us. Annie would rattle into the middle of nowhere, so we thought we'd be the first Chinese ever there, only to find some stone wall built by them or some cellar chiseled out of solid rock. And we'd realize that we weren't pioneers at all.

And just when I thought we were the only Asians for hundreds of miles, a Chinese would show up at our game. I couldn't help thinking that those three old funny Guests had gotten the word out on the grapevine.

If we happened to stumble on a Chinese restaurant or laundry, we could expect a free hot meal and a floor to sleep on. Otherwise, because money was short, we slept in the car.

Yet, despite the hungry nights and the long trips and miserable wages, I wouldn't have traded a moment of it. I never felt alone again, because I knew we six were all in it together. Or maybe even seven. Despite our harsh parting, I found myself thinking of Jack whenever I used some tip he had taught me.

After every game, Topper struck another town from the list until we rolled into Moab. There, we were going to play the Harlem Globetrotters themselves.

CHAPTER | XV

We'd never been in an auditorium as big as the one in Moab, and we'd never had a crowd like that. Through the walls of the locker room, we could hear the excitement build outside—a rumbling like locomotives stoking up their boilers for a race. And when we went outside, there were literally people hanging from the rafters so they could get a better view. And though it was bitterly cold outside that night, it was as hot as a steam bath inside from all the bodies.

Barney grinned at me nervously. "So Topper's fans have turned out tonight."

"Sure," I cracked. "They want to see Topper's legs."

We started to warm up. There were some bored folks who watched us because we were the only thing to see, but most of the crowd just kept yakking away, so we might as well have been sweeping the floor as shooting baskets.

The roar was deafening when the Globetrotters came in, and I found myself looking at them from the corner of my eye. They were all smiles as they began passing the ball around—whipping it from one to the other as casually as if they were tossing a hat. And when the ball touched a hand, it looked as if it were glued there until they tossed it to the next. The trick dribbles and passes were just so amazing that we all stopped to gawk like everyone else.

One guy was a regular magician who could make the basketball come alive, as if it were his pet. He made it travel up one arm, over his shoulders, and then down the other arm, and he could juggle three basketballs as easily as if they were oranges.

Topper was the only one of us who had seen the Globetrotters before. He jerked his head at the wizard. "That's Ted Strong."

I felt my belly begin to spin, just as Strong was doing with a basketball on his fingertip. I was going to have my hands full.

Topper was looking even grimmer than when Jack had left us. "Everyone's got to play their best game tonight because if they get too far ahead, they'll start doing that to us during the game."

"That seems kinda insulting," Alphonse said. I think practical jokers hated it the most when pranks were played on them.

"I don't think they mean to do that to the other team." Topper set a hand on his hip as he watched some particularly tricky ballhandling. "It's just that a lot of times the score gets so lopsided that the crowd gets bored. So they need to find some way to keep the fans interested. They'll keep coming back for a good show as well as for a good game."

"So they're in the entertainment business as much as sports," the Professor said.

Hollywood elbowed him sharply in the ribs. "Now you're sounding like Jack."

The Professor was watching their big man, whom Topper said was Bernie Price.

"Well, we're on our own now. We got to think of that side of things," he said.

"Where's Jack?" a short man asked as he strolled over toward us.

"He quit," Topper said. "The inmates are running the asylum now."

The short man blinked in surprise but then recovered quick enough to extend his hand. "Abe. Abe Saperstein. I helped book your tour." He had the grin of a natural-born salesman.

"It's a killer," Alphonse moaned, and pretended to bend over as if he were carrying a ton of scrap iron.

Abe slapped him on the back. "Don't let my guys hear that or they'll laugh. One year we played two hundred and thirty games. We wore out four sets of tires. *Your* schedule would seem like a vacation to them."

I winced, feeling sorry for the Globetrotters, but Topper looked intrigued. "No kidding?" He glared at us. "The ball's not going to go into the hoop by itself. Start shooting." And then he and Abe strolled off for a chat—a lot of smiles and laughs on Abe's part and a lot of thoughtful nods on Topper's.

"Topper's always got an angle too," Hollywood said as he took his set shot.

I would have liked to watch more of the Globetrotters' show, but I turned to the others. "The last thing I want is to be the butt of their jokes."

"Amen to that," Alphonse muttered, and from the determined expressions on the others' mugs, I knew they were thinking the same thing.

We went back to warming up, but we were so tense with worry that the balls we threw kept clanging on the rim and bouncing back. If we shot like this during the game, it was going to be the longest and most humiliating night of our lives.

When we went back to the bench, Topper had finished his chat with Abe, so we huddled around him. "I think we're catching the Globetrotters at the right time." A newspaper guy, Hearst, had started a World Professional Tournament last year with $10,000 in prizes and bragging rights for the winner, and he had invited all the top professional teams, including the House of David, the Celtics, the best of the National Basketball League teams, the Globetrotters, and the Rens. The Rens was short for the New York Renaissance, the team on which the Globetrotters had patterned themselves and in whose shadow they had played for years. After challenging the Rens to a match for a long time, the Globetrotters had gotten their chance last March but lost to them—27 to 23.

Topper figured they would want revenge this year. "They're probably looking beyond us to the big tournament. But I don't care how tall or fast they are. We can take these guys if we push it up."

Alphonse looked over his shoulder at the Globetrotters crowded around Abe, but in contrast to our tense selves, they were relaxed and joking with one another.

"I'll just be happy if we can keep the score close," he said, echoing all our sentiments.

Topper jabbed him sharply in the chest with stiff fingers. "Losers talk like that. We're winners. We can take on the whole world. I'm not going back to Chinatown with my tail between my legs like some beaten dog."

Hollywood eyed Topper skeptically. "You got some strategy, coach?"

"Yeah, put the ball into the hoop a lot," Topper grunted, and promptly sat down on the bench. I was surprised that he didn't start the game, but after the first tip-off I was resentful because I thought he was trying to avoid the humiliation.

We'd met tall teams before, but none of them, not even the Davids, could run and shoot like the Globetrotters. I thought I could handle a ball, but I was a lummox next to Ted Strong. He had the biggest hands I'd ever seen—and the quickest. I only caught glimpses of the ball, and when I did, it was just a blur. And even when I had my back to him while I dribbled, somehow the ball disappeared from my hand and the next thing I knew he was lobbing it to a man streaking to the other basket. Make a mistake with him and *whoosh!* Another two points for the Globetrotters.

By the end of the quarter, we were down by ten, and it was clear they could sink a basket anytime they wanted.

We were all feeling pretty discouraged when we trudged back to the bench during a time-out. My legs were feeling wobbly from chasing Strong back and forth because Topper had left me in the whole time.

"Now I know how those other teams felt playing us," Barney said with a groan.

I was dreading the moment when they would start playing their pranks on us. That moment couldn't be very far away now.

Topper had us huddle around him and, after shedding his jacket, he started to rattle off the moves and even little tics and leg twitches that would tip us off to what each Globetrotter was going to do.

Despite the heat inside the auditorium, I was so sweaty that I was feeling cold, so I put on my jacket. "You were scouting them from the bench?"

"Why else would I let you botch my plays?" Topper asked as he bounced up and down on the balls of his feet and then did some quick stretches. "Watch and learn, kid."

Topper had kept the gears turning in his brain just like Jack had told me to do—only I'd been so scared that I'd forgotten.

By some miracle, the Professor got the tip-off and Topper began bawling to push it up. We got a basket before they could set up. All too soon, the Globetrotters figured out how we were anticipating their moves, but by that point, Topper's clues had helped us cut their lead to just five.

After that, whether it was defense or offense, Topper kept us running full bore, and though their legs must have been hurting as much as mine, they did it.

Of course, man for man in quickness, strength, and reach, the Globetrotters were still better than us. However, we had the satisfaction of wiping the relaxed smiles from their faces, and they kept playing us seriously. They knew that if they started to fool around, they might lose.

When the second half started and I trotted out, Topper whispered to me, "Now let's show them the real Flash because we need him now."

Praise from Topper? I glanced at him in surprise, but he was already moving toward his man.

Buoyed by Topper's vote of confidence, I took up my position by Ted Strong. As soon as he saw me, the tension left his shoulders—he probably figured he was going to make another easy meal out of me and maybe he was already planning one of his clowning tricks just to show me who was boss. Their big man, Bernie Price, got the tip-off, and I started to back-pedal immediately in a line to intercept Strong since I figured he was going to get the ball.

He dashed toward me, but I was ready for his fake and I thrust out my arm, anticipating where the ball was going to be as he dribbled. Actually, I never saw it, so I was lucky I didn't foul him; but it was a triumphant moment when my palm slapped against something round and hard and then the ball was bouncing away.

I shot past him toward it. From the corner of my eye, I saw Alphonse breaking for the other basket and batted the ball toward him. I felt just like a kid at Christmas when I saw him put it through the net.

I can't say that I won any more battles against Strong because he stopped taking me for granted, but I made him work as hard as the rest of the Globetrotters. No pranks. No fooling around. Just straight basketball. As Jack had said, there was more to winning than just the scoreboard.

By the end of the game, we'd chopped the score down to a respectable three-point loss, and the crowd went away feeling as satisfied as we were.

"Nice game, kid," Ted Strong grinned afterward and stuck out his hand.

"Thanks. The name's Cal—I mean, Flash. Flash Chin." When we shook hands, I felt as if he'd wrapped mine in a baseball glove.

He winked. "Are you as tired as I feel, Flash? Man, oh, man, I hope Abe never schedules you again."

I didn't believe him for a moment, but I appreciated his kindness.

And Abe Saperstein paid us the compliment of coming over and asking to taste what was in our teakettle. He took a sip and swirled it around on his tongue as if he were sampling a fine wine. We all laughed when he made a face. "Ugh, I can't stand tea without cream and sugar." He wiped his mouth with the back of one hand. "I figured you must have some kind of magic juice in there to give my guys such a hard time."

In a nice, teasing way, he said other things that made us feel good too. I could see how he had built the Globetrotters into a moneymaking machine because he could have charmed the moon out of the sky and sold it for cheese.

Because the advance ticket sales had been so good, we could afford a hotel and had already made our reservations, though we all had to share one room. The place was a real dive like the others that were willing to rent to us, but it would still be a luxury to sleep in a room with four plaster walls instead of Annie's metal sides.

As it happened, the Globetrotters were staying there too, so our two cars made a little convoy back there. But when we got out, they started to head down the alley past the garbage cans.

"Where are you going?" I called to Ted Strong.

"We have to use the service entrance." His shrug said it all. These were the greatest basketball players I'd ever seen, but that wasn't enough to get them through the front door. Then he lifted his head. "But it won't always be that way."

To his credit, Abe led the way to the back door.

I felt both sad and angry at the same time as I watched them trudge away.

Barney glanced nervously at the hotel. "Maybe we should use the service entrance too."

"We're going through the front door," Topper insisted.

"We're too much of a novelty," the Professor explained. "Fifty years ago we probably couldn't have even stayed at a dump like this, but then the Americans drove most of the Chinese out, so six of us won't be a threat—especially since we're leaving tomorrow."

We were all a little tense when we went into the lobby. The bored desk clerk had turned on a radio, so I could hear Louis Armstrong singing and playing a muted trumpet. I wondered if Armstrong would have been allowed in the lobby if he were here in person.

We froze when the desk clerk suddenly waved at us. I thought he was going to tell us to go around back, but he asked, "Is one of you Calvin Chin?"

"That's me," I said.

He held up a little yellow envelope. "You got a telegram."

It was the first one I'd ever gotten and I hoped it would be my last. Barney took one look at my face and said, "What's wrong?"

"He's dead," I said.

Barney took the telegram and glanced through it. "I'm sorry."

I tried to shrug it off. "It was only a matter of time before the booze or the loan sharks got to him."

"Hey, why the long face, kid?" Alphonse called, but he stopped when Barney shook his head.

I just stood there while Barney held a quick whispered conversation with the rest of the team. Funny, all my life I wished I'd been free of the old man. He'd been nothing but an albatross around my neck ever since I was born, and yet I felt tears stinging the corners of my eyes.

Then the team huddled around me. Hands clasped my shoulders and arms and I heard all the words of sympathy, but those words are more for the speaker than the mourner. They were just sounds to me.

Finally Topper eased me from the middle. "Let's go for a walk, kid."

I wanted to be alone, but I didn't have the energy to tell him that, so I let him guide me out of the hotel and back into the quiet town. We kept silent for a couple of blocks, him strolling, me stumbling.

Then he cleared his throat. "I lost my dad five years ago, so I know what you're feeling."

"No, you don't," I snapped. "I bet people missed your dad. Mine left nothing but a trail of heartaches and IOU's behind him."

"From what I hear, you took care of him," Topper said. "There had to be something worthwhile inside him. Maybe not when he got older, but maybe when you were smaller."

"Don't you think I've tried to remember something nice?" I shot back. "But I couldn't come up with one memory." I gave a snort. "He even stole my lunch money when my mom's back was turned." But then why did I feel such an ache inside me?

When we returned to the room we were all sharing, I saw the others lying on the floor. Topper gave me a nudge. "The bed's all yours tonight, kid."

"You deserve it, not me," I said.

"Consider it a late Christmas present from us," Topper said, curling up on the floorboards with the others.

I didn't bother undressing. I just kicked off my shoes and climbed into the sack, but sleep wouldn't come.

Sometimes I thought about how my father had never seen me play the game. If I hadn't taken any pride in him, he hadn't taken any in me either. It was mutual contempt.

Other times I thought about the Globetrotters having to use the back door. I thought about the long road they had already traveled to build up loving crowds like the one they had here, and yet they still had to use the service entrance in the meanest dive.

I couldn't say which made me feel worse. Once again, I wished Jean were here. She could always help me set my thoughts straight.

CHAPTER | XVI

"The next day when we got to the town and the gym where we were going to play next, Topper told me I could sit out the game that night, but I said I wanted to play.

"You don't have to," Topper assured me. "We've managed with five before."

"Barney'd be okay, but you four old geezers are just one step away from heart attacks," I objected.

"I can still outrun and outshoot you," he insisted.

But I was feeling all wild and reckless inside, and there was still something unsettled between us. "Prove it. Let's have another game of twenty-one."

Topper hesitated. "We should save our energy for the game."

"Scared I'm going to take back my jersey?" I challenged.

Topper's eyes narrowed. "No way."

The team lounged around on the benches while Topper and I marched to one end of the gym. It was a relief to get on the court because, with all the complexities of the game, basketball was still a lot simpler than life. You just have to put the ball through the hoop, and the rules on how you could do it were neat and clear. Living with people was a lot harder.

Topper tried to pull his usual tricks, but by now I'd seen all of them. And thanks to Jack's teaching, I wasn't the same playground kid he had whipped in that first game. When the score was tied at thirteen, I could see the uncertainty in his eyes just like I'd seen in the eyes of opponents in dozens of other games.

By now, we both had the feeling that we were playing for more than the jersey. At stake was the leadership of the team. So he came at me even harder and threw in a couple of things he hadn't used before, but after all these games I knew how to recover from a surprise. And when we were still tied at nineteen, I could see the panic set in. And that was sweet.

I was panting, but he was panting even more. He tried his best to keep up with me, but he couldn't overcome the fact that my legs were younger. Still, he didn't give up. When I leaped up for the final winning basket, he tried to jump with me, but he was just too tired.

He didn't even bother turning around to see if I'd made it. He could tell by the swish of the ball through the net. No one cheered. The Dragons were silent—as if they were at a funeral.

It was the moment I'd been waiting for since the tour had started, so I should have felt triumphant, but I felt just like the rest of the team. Topper and I would never be best friends, but we'd been through so much together and I'd come to count on him on this long, hard road.

Without a word, he began to take off his jersey. "Here, kid. You earned it."

I stopped him. "No," I said. "I know it means a lot to you. So keep it."

"Don't do it because you feel sorry for me," he said softly.

"You dope, don't you know respect when you see it?" I asked, and then I jerked my thumb toward our teammates. "Besides, who wants to be in charge of those mugs?"

He gave me a grateful nod and then pretended to be stern. "Only a lazybones would leave all the work to someone else."

"That's me, all right," I agreed, wondering how either of us was going to get through the game tonight after our hard-fought contest. And as it turned out, we lost, but at least not by much.

We made it through the rest of the tour and when the weather turned better, we even started making a little profit to split, so everybody was feeling pretty good in

March as we chugged across the upper deck of the Bay Bridge toward San Francisco. Below us on the lower deck the electric cars of the Key System rattled and clicked, and then we headed off the bridge into the shadowy canyons between the city's skyscrapers.

As we finally clattered into Chinatown, Alphonse twisted his head as he looked left and right. "Nothing's changed."

"Except us," the Professor murmured.

Topper let us off near Tiger's place because Jean had sent me a postcard in another package that had told me all my stuff was stored there. Ah Lee hadn't waited long to reclaim his storeroom, and I couldn't blame him. He probably needed to fumigate it. And he was probably pretty sore that my old man had died inside his store and scared off some of his more superstitious customers.

Topper got out and stretched. "So if I can scrape up the dough, want to try again next year?"

"Heck, yes," Barney said without hesitating.

"We'll really do it up right this time." Topper slapped the fender. "I'll get us a big-size touring car, even if it means going into hock."

"Replace Annie? She's one of the team too," Hollywood protested from inside.

"Yeah, what was I thinking?" Topper laughed. "Okay, we'll fix the old gal up and give her a paint job too. And new uniforms for us—real robes of red silk. They'll look good under the lights." He looked beyond us as if he were already seeing us in a gym. "There's big things ahead for us. One of these days we'll be in that tournament taking on the Rens and Globetrotters."

"You can count on me," Barney promised eagerly.

Topper glanced at me because I hadn't said a word and then turned back to Barney. "Okay, talk to your partner." He grinned. "And to your agents. Got to keep the team together."

He got into Annie again and she gave a loud, sassy *a-rooga* as she sashayed back into the traffic. It was her way of saying "See you next year."

As people passed by, ignoring us, I sighed. "No banners. No bands. No parades. We're back to being nobodies."

"Alphonse is wrong. Chinatown looks smaller," Barney said, and wriggled his shoulders. "Like it's a shirt that I outgrew and now it's too tight."

"You're turning into another Professor," I warned with a laugh.

"Naw, my noggin's so tiny that an idea'd have to have a magnifying glass to find it," Barney chuckled. "Say, what are you going to do tonight? You want to sleep at Grandpa Joe's?"

I blinked because I'd slept in Annie so often that I'd gotten used to thinking of her as my home. "Just for a few nights until I find a place of my own." Thanks to Jean and Grandpa Joe's foresight, I knew I had some money in the bank. "And thanks. You're a good friend."

Barney winked. "We're teammates, right?"

We picked up our bags and headed into the dimly lit tenement. Loud noises came from the apartments on each floor. And I began to feel just like Barney: Chinatown, my old home, was too small and confining for us.

Grandpa Joe had known that when he had first suggested I join the team. I thought again of the Guests and how folks like Grandpa Joe had spread out through America, and then how the troubles had come and the Chinese had retreated into places like Chinatown. But it was time to go back outside—despite the landlords who didn't want to rent to you and the threats and the other bad stuff that could happen. And Barney and me and the team had been part of it. There was a whole country to explore again.

As we climbed the steps, I wondered if Jack was home, or even if he had a home. Wherever he was, I wished him well. Then I looked behind me at Barney. "Tell Tops that if he can get the scratch together, I'll go again."

The radio was on loud. Jack Benny was torturing his violin again, but somebody heard our knock and jerked the door open. Warm, moist air rushed out of the apartment, carrying delicious smells.

Little Phil squinted up at us. "You made it back." It sounded like an accusation.

"Sorry, squirt, we should've tried harder not to," Barney said. He ruffled Phil's hair and Phil glared back at him and straightened it.

"Kill the fatted calf," I called, "the prodigals have returned." Seeing how much Phil hated it, I mussed up his hair for good measure.

Tiger jumped up from the table, and I felt my own heart skip when I saw Jean there too, but my tongue got all clumsy.

"Got the packages," I mumbled. "Thanks."

"The whole team wants to marry you," Barney said.

"That's nice," Jean sniffed.

Tiger's mother shuffled out of the kitchen. "Hello, hello!" she said, and gave each of us big hugs.

Barney sniffed the air and rubbed his stomach. "Something's cooking on the stove."

"Jook, of course," Phil scowled. "I'm getting tired of it."

Tiger laughed. "Mom's been keeping it going all this time just waiting for you."

"And doughnuts?" Barney asked hopefully.

Tiger's mom looked at Tiger and Jean, who both nodded.

"You're done, so it's okay," Jean said.

Barney glanced at me but didn't say anything about the possible new tour. He didn't want to lose those doughnuts.

Tiger was so happy to have him back that she didn't notice, but Jean did. "What's wrong?"

"Nothing," I said, and tried to change the subject hurriedly. "How's the job going?"

Tiger frowned. "Jean won't complain, but they just promoted this girl who came in after her and who dumps all her work on Jean's desk."

She didn't have to say what skin color the girl had. It was an old story in Chinatown.

"With your brains and drive, you ought to be the manager," I said angrily.

"It's a steady paycheck," Jean smiled mischievously. "But when I have to make six duplicates of a letter, I pretend the keys are my boss and I pound away. Every copy comes out real clear, but I go through typewriter ribbons like crazy."

Jean had her own battles just like I had, but she hadn't complained in any of her postcards. As usual, I'd been so caught up in myself that I hadn't asked her how she was doing.

I gulped and tried to say more, but by then, Tiger's little brothers and sisters were clamoring to hear more about our trip. In the general hubbub, Jean whispered to me, "What was that look Barney gave you?"

"Talk about it later," I said.

"You bet we will," Jean said.

Tiger's mom got out her jade necklace for the occasion and put it on with what she announced was her formal attire and then sat down at the head of the table.

Everybody stuffed themselves on jook and doughnuts, and of course Tiger's mom had to hear all the details of our trip, so Barney had to tell them all over again.

I left all the talking to him because it cut down on his time for scarfing down doughnuts and gave me a fair shot at them.

Jean didn't say much either. She just picked bits off her doughnut and rolled them between her fingertips into little pills on her plate. "Um, you want that doughnut?" I asked, since it seemed to be going to waste.

"Why don't you eat it while we take a walk?" she suggested. She was already rising. "I should tell you about your father, and we don't want to spoil the party."

Silence instantly fell around the table. "I have your boxes under the bed," Tiger's mother said.

I didn't see how she could have squeezed one more thing into her place, but I thanked her.

"And don't worry about the funeral," Tiger assured me. "Grandpa Joe got your family association to kick in for it."

"They probably wanted to make sure my old man was dead," I said.

Tiger's mom reached over the table and rapped my forehead with her knuckles—quick, efficient, hard—like the expert she was. "Don't talk like that." She settled back in her chair. "And make sure you write a thank-you letter to them."

I wasn't about to risk losing any more of her doughnuts, so I promised dutifully. Jean disappeared into the
bedroom and came out a moment later with a flat package under her arm. "Come on."

"Uh, yeah, thanks," I said to Tiger and her mother.
"Nice to be home again."

"You want the couch or the floor at Grandpa Joe's?"
Barney asked. He'd dug out a coin to toss for it.

"I'll take the floor," I said, waving off the bet.
Barney had such bad luck at gambling that he probably
would have lost the coin toss, and he really deserved
the couch.

When Jean and I stepped outside, I heard some swing
band in the distance in one of the night-clubs doing a
good imitation of Benny Goodman's rouser, "Sing, Sing,
Sing." It always made me want to tap my feet, but it didn't
seem like the proper moment.

It's funny, but I had thought over and over about what
would happen when I was alone with Jean: how I'd tell her
how much she meant to me. Only now that the moment
had arrived, I couldn't find the words. "Uh, thanks for
taking care of my old man," I said lamely.

"It was a team effort between Grandpa Joe, Tiger,
Tiger's mom, and me," she said. "We made sure he had
meals and money."

"Sorry you had to go through all that," I said. I
knew that whatever he got would have been, in his
opinion, smaller than he deserved and that he would

have cried, raged, cursed, and begged—all in the space of ten minutes—and then lost himself in a bottle.

She eyed me. "Whatever you say, don't tell me it was what *pals* do."

"No," I admitted. "That went way beyond friendship."

She thrust the package at me. "Here. He wanted you to have this."

"My inheritance?" I started to joke, but I saw her face and swallowed the wisecracks. I slid it out of the pillowcase—it was old but clean. I bet he made poor Jean wash it for him. I saw it was a scrapbook. It was as classy as they came, with a cover of red satin and silk cords. As I turned the pages, I saw photographs and articles.

"Where'd he get these?" I asked.

"Jack sent them," Jean said. "Didn't you know?"

"No," I said, turning the pages. But there were articles even from the games after Jack had left. "Where'd these come from?"

"Some of Grandpa Joe's friends," Jean said. She brushed some hair from her eyes as she peered at the pages with me.

The articles about our games were from all over the country. "I don't know how they got their hands on them."

"Probably other friends." Jean shrugged. "You'd have to ask them."

"I was going to keep them, but your dad asked for them," Jean explained. "He's the one who got the scrapbook and put them in."

I couldn't see him spending money on anything but booze. "You got to be kidding."

"He was proud of you," Jean said.

I was dumbfounded. Wherever my name was mentioned, he'd underlined it. "He could've written me himself."

"He wasn't good at talking about his feelings," Jean said. "His son isn't any better."

"I really, really appreciate it," I said uncomfortably. "But at least on the next tour you won't have to handle him anymore." I told her briefly about Topper's plan. "There won't be much money either this time. But I'd like to keep you as my agent."

"Is that all?" She glared up at me. "It's no fun being taken for granted, you know."

I only seemed to be making her madder and madder. I felt even more helpless than I had against the Globetrotters. It was hopeless.

"Yeah, well," I mumbled. "Maybe we ought to break up then." I felt tears beginning to squeeze their way out of the corners of my eyes.

Jean sucked in her breath. "Is that it?"

I turned away so she couldn't see me crying. "It's the best thing for you. I'm just a basketball bum."

She grabbed my arm and swung me around. "That's not what I think." She touched her fingers to my wet cheek to brush away a tear. "That's not what Tiger's family thinks. Or Barney or Grandpa Joe. Or your team."

"But you handled my old man. You saw what he was like," I said. "I'm not going to be any better."

"It's not like you to quit, Cal." Jean swung her head toward the music playing in the next nightclub. "Do you think I like working all day? I'd like to go out and have fun as much as the next person. I just try to be the best person I can be. On court, you're a special person; you're Flash. So try to be as special off court too."

I scratched my head. "Man, you're good at pep talks. So you're a coach as well as an agent. You make me feel like I could do it."

"Of course you can," she said. "You've got people rooting for you, Cal."

"I'll need my agent and coach, though," I said, tapping her chin.

"I'll be there," she promised. And I knew she would.

I looked up at the sky; the buildings here were squeezed together so tight I couldn't see anything up above us.

"I wish you could've seen the moon like it was out there. It was just so big and bright."

She laughed and pointed at the street lamp. "It'll have to do."

So we kissed under its light.

AFTERWORD

As teenagers in the 1930s, my family and their friends had the same amusements as their white counterparts, but because of racial barriers they usually held their dances, played tennis, basketball, football, and even learned fencing among other things within the confines of Chinatown. This novel is drawn not only from their sports stories but from their memories of the Great Depression itself: Johnny Kan's five-cent bread loaves, the smell of coffee beans roasting at the Hills Brothers plant on the Embarcadero (a popular brand in Chinatown as a result), the fund-raising parades with the gigantic Chinese flag, and even the rumors about the Japanese storekeepers—are all from their reminiscences. Calvin's experiences in job hunting are drawn from my father's own during that awful time.

"Uncle" George Lee had been a close friend of my parents. He had coached my mother's basketball team, the Mei Wahs, and later as a newlywed he and his wife had played hearts with my parents, the winning couple using the winnings to treat the losing couple to a late evening snack at a restaurant.

He had run the Hong Wah Kues as the player-owner during the second tour in 1940. Abe Saperstein helped schedule their games, but his relationship with the team did not extend beyond that. In his conciliatory letter replying to Uncle George's complaints about the scheduling, Abe Saperstein certainly did not take the tone of an owner speaking to an employee.

In 1987, I was able to interview Uncle George and look at his scrapbook, reading the clippings about their game in Kellogg, Idaho. He was proud that his team had played there. He also told me about the incident with the bad tires. However, unlike my story, their manager bought new tires and the strike was averted.

I was also able to examine some posters from the team's game, including the one advertising a game against a team called the Native Americans. I was surprised to see that phrase being used as early as 1939–1940, but that was the name that was printed in large letters.

Another poster came from a game against the House of David. Uncle George described the game with relish, including the Davids' threat and subsequent punishment when the Hong Wah Kues began winning. It is also from him that I heard about the three old Guests who kept swapping deeds in a remote Chinatown and the threatened strike over worn-out tires—though it was resolved with less fireworks.

The game against the Native Americans was drawn from Fred Kuo's interview with my niece, Dr. Kathleen S. Yep, in her forthcoming book on Chinese American sports, *Outside the Paint: Embodied Pedagogy and the Politics of Chinatown Basketball, 1930–1950*. However, the Ring Man and what happened to him are imaginary.

Similarly, the descriptions of the game against the Harlem Globetrotters were drawn from my conversation with "Uncle" George Lee, who relished the compliment from the Globetrotter after the game. He did not name the Globetrotter so I attributed it to Ted Strong, who was featured in articles from the same local papers. The chapter was also supplemented by Dr. Yep's book.

Again, I want to stress that though this book is based upon actual events, the story and the characters are fictional. The same characters reappear in other books from the Golden Mountain Chronicles. *Sea Glass* describes Calvin and Jean's later family and other books in the Golden Mountain Chronicles, *Child of the Owl* and *Thief of Hearts*, deal with Barney and Tiger's children and grandchildren. Grandpa Joe's earlier life in Rock Springs, Wyoming, is described in *The Traitor*.

My family and their friends have been a constant source of inspiration to me. Despite all the obstacles they faced, they never stopped hoping and dreaming and working toward their goals, and their example has constantly encouraged me to keep trying to tell their stories.

BIBLIOGRAPHY

Though there are many books and articles on modern basketball, there are not as many on basketball from this period, but here are a few:

Harris, Ron. "Hoops Pioneer Hank Luisetti Dies at 86." *San Francisco Chronicle*, December 22, 2002.

Lapchick, Joe. *50 Years of Basketball*. Englewood Cliffs, New Jersey: Prentice-Hall, 1968.

Nolte, Carl. "Slam-Dunk Memories: 60 years ago, Chinatown had its own pro basketball team." *San Francisco Chronicle*, May 28, 1999.

Peterson, Robert W. *Cages to Jump Shots: Pro Basketball's Early Years*. New York, Oxford: Oxford University Press, 1990.

Yep, Dr. Kathleen Susan. *Outside the Paint: Embodied Pedagogy and the Politics of Chinatown Basketball, 1930–1950* (forthcoming).